A CREATION PRESS SAMPLER

“CEASE TO EXIST”

A Creation Press Sampler

ISBN 1 871592 07 0

CREATION PRESS
83, Clerkenwell Road
London EC1
071-430-9878

CONTENTS

"CATHEDRAL LUNG"

Aaron Williamson

Reveal the cosmogenic intricacies of the cathedral.

Layers heave an internal web, dead wheels of fortune churn, in urgency, hysterical, a saffron sun in cycle with the trinities of freaks splashed out at intersecting grids and networks; writhing, flashing.

Molecules burn out. A substrate warm mosaic transforms the panic into optical sensations, these accompanied by manacled anguishes of suffocation.

Transparent grating sounds screeching impeccably. A thread of panes cross-sect precise disembodiments of frost as swollen developments of insects colonise the permeable clamour.

Inside the stellar vagus vault, the flayed tongue is painted with menstrual flake. A gong is pulverised.

The silence begins.

Breathing balanced the slab in the air. Soul is on every hand. This lethal silence dreaming a waning vaporous crescent heaven.

A lung is formed by walls of rotting stone. Seeming to emanate from feeble wavering beams, the lung bleeds over an array of deep damp moss through which can be distinguished rows of overgrown facades, all crumbling.

The rotting stone associates the picture of decrepitude and the signs seared into the hour have all been long crescent moons of centuries.

Hollow frangible old slabs, urns repellant with rank grass and weeds suggest cavities luring curiosity. Within lie catacombs, immense years nibbling the arcades of tangible refractions.

Creatures invade, high in the moon-peered valley's rim; squares peel along the edges, corrosion, herding the quicksilver.

The cranial bone. Sharpened flints. The scribbling

lines across the dome are ridges of bone built up in those places where stresses occur.

This is being eaten from within. This is not a heart drumming into the table but the sound of a devouring agent located in the craw.

Taken from "CATHEDRAL LUNG".

"CACOPHONIES"

Aaron Williamson

#7

Winged
demon dimmer down
beneath skies tugging
the avatar, the atom
blur:
father son or papaboy
cauterized and slit
amongst the ganglia
for drainage
of the roly-poly ghost
cloyed and
clubbing into the life-bank;
an old penny-measurer
hacking
the anaesthetic
ashcan lipids:
"it wants to come out,
to breathe forth
- it needs to..."
there's a cadaver
advancing in the radial,
the bike vaults
breaking, deluging
like a skeleton
but glued together from dust
and poking at the tensiles
of the earth
to help them slack
and flood:
beating at the streaming raptures
sparks wrenched
welded
upon the dampened floors
around a sacral heart.

#12

A gelatine of crushed stars
suspended
into a boiling spectrum
of crevices
and hanging by a thread of nerve,
sledgehammering
the blood, meat and bone;
the bronze columns
of a palamino machette
collapsing
hacking
the sphery platform into
four separate planes:
heart hand and foot
but four separate planes which
feign
to be collapsed...
fac fal
fac fal
fac fallo
it's facial, fatal,
a committed facialist
"I resist the glacialist
dock"
like money runs up the clock
pissed,
as a vat of blood
slaps the head
of a vat of blood
and sledehammers a scum surface
apotheosis
of the merely dimensional
(on four separate planes)
in order to flight
a canopy
of glittering sidereal:
a nebular body
dragged up

from the skin pavements
like a kicked-up galaxy of limbs;
“no kidding...”

"DEAR SURGEON"

Aaron Williamson

Dear surgeon,

the operation takes place
at night
within the chancel
of a well-known cathedral:
the intention,
in physical terms,
is to approximate the conditions
occurring
under a profound freezing
surgery:
a block of concrete
houses a single vibrating reed
and this constitutes
my voice.

I have no fingers,
only a part;
a particle that is
stitched into reality
somewhere inside
approaching the root
of the tongue.

And the closer you get
to this point,
the more, that is,
that you turn back
into it
in order to taste
the very substance
of its inner marrow;
the more you realise,
or "make real",

the finality
that this tongue
emits no language;
that is is, in fact,
an organ misappropriated
into a function
for which it never was
intended.

Those who know,
they do not speak.

"I cried unto god
with my voice,
even
unto god
with my voice
and it gave ear
unto me"

Taken from "CATHEDRAL LUNG".

"FREEDOM, LIBERTY AND TINSEL"

Aaron Williamson

This shit hole desert with its ghosts watch International Terrorism prepare to gently press the detonator as the hot breath of death blasts everything into a stomach of iron filings.

International grinned sourly, towards the viewer, towards the cactus lined horizon where the world is filled with innocent victims potentially. Like a caged animal, the frenzied air-conditioning couldn't keep from sweating. Shit hole desert. His hand, once moulded to the shape of gun metal now floats, with the purpling bruises, the innate beauty, through a wide arc in space.

Only the edge of a knife-edge of caged hysteria.

*****

Death is shaking, it is shaking in alleyways and Paraguays, the chillin' hands of death descend to shake the creepin' fleas out-of-it-all: O Fol de Rolio; like screaming through the streets pursued by rips and cracks, the crumbling paraffinhalia of civilisation collapsing, curling-in towards its own back: De Rolio, no skin, no skin nor foolish truths to hide behind, just snakes-for-veins and flash eruptions of blood amongst the traffic O look right: Hell hath no fire escape; and right again: heaven rents no step ladders...merely a string of man-made razor blades is tossed into the squirming pit of brotherhood, equality etcetera...

*****

Existence has no exit
bulbed up on fuckout,
snapped out of exits
eviled out of I-head;
what am I doing here?
- I found out at last;
I was an ex-It,
simply a do-nut hole torn out of the sky
through which the coming dawn
commuters form
explosions of birds goin'
think I'd scorch my wings??

- well I could die
just for opening my mouth
I mean speaking such shit
I mean be killed by Satan and HIS sidekick
- I'm no buddah,
I'm a wanker:
Buddah can you spare me a dimension?
How clever. Wanker.
Or just a mention?
- upon the smooth floor of galaxies...

You see?
I have with me, at all times,
the magic words
with which to form a sentence of death.
Of course, I can't SAY them,
they're not playthings
...I grew a flower that filled me with tears;
feathers upon my teeth,
my nerves were sticking out HERE
far enough to form wings:
a pair of clipped and soiled wings
that flap but never get me in the air:

I do nothing, I go nowhere, I see no-one.

think I'd scorch my wings?

*****

The thugbaby sits in the corner
shaking the thugbaby's rattle
I mean something that feels like a
thug or a baby
or a battery of bats:
overhead
two broken nude bodies cling
to the ceiling with magnets
as the thugbaby stares
in the electric fire.
He imagines I imagine being born
in front of it,
our arms shot through
with welding rods,
copper wire,
nailed down
to the floorboards at angles,
waiting
for someone on the next floor down
with pliers...
through the ceiling;
anything.
In the meantime, the thugbaby
sees energy laugh,
laughing in the electric fire:
he is switched on,
STIFFENS.
The neighbours go out.
THUd.
One broken nude body
drops to the pulsating carpet
around the thugbaby's ears.

Taken from "CATHEDRAL LUNG".

"BEATING THE MEAT"

Tony Reed

A slaughterhouse is a sexual place; it has its own courtship rituals, its own dark consummations. The odours in bed and blood-gutter, the sounds of passion and pain aren't, after all, so very different. Think: if orgasm is a little death, how much greater the release of that grander end? How unremarkable, then, that so many cattle meet that ultimate moment with engorged cock or dripping cunt.

Their anticipation comes as a special vibration, a thrill of fear and longing travelling up through the jumping cold sacramental steel of the humane killer, even as its captive bolt stabs down. One hundred, two hundred times a day, I grant absolution in a tethered silver bullet, a death of quicksilver fire in my hand, punching a message of eternity into the skulls of shivering beasts. Their eyes roll in their orbits, in supplication or distress; their legs buckle and they kneel, lowing or squealing in voices made suddenly human. They die. Hear that sound once, and you will never forget it, a crying which imprints itself on the deepest chambers of your heart. A cry of outrage and acceptance. The sound of *your* death in violence. And I am the one that grants it. The slaughterman.

Born to the work: inherited from my father, anticipated from my youth. Brought up with the flat copper scent of gore in my nostrils, the taste of juice-oozing flesh stuffing my mouth Childhood was an education in the thousand secret cuts of bleeding, gutting, and filleting. And an education, too, in the keener cuts, which go deeper, and are not felt at all.

Scene from a pre-school day. I wait for Father by the front gate, at the limit of my permitted world, hopping with impatience and the futile desire to see beyond the low (not low enough!) brick wall, down this quiet suburban road to where he must first appear. From behind curtains, grey and indistinct, comes the policing voice of Mother, irritation without threat, a nuisance only, which might drown out the first faint indicators of his return.

"Richard? Richard! Don't you dare open that gate now, do you hear? And stop hopping about so. You'll dirty your clothes. Richard, are you listening to me?"

I ignore her. For now, right *now* I can hear him, whistling randomly as he always does, exchanging greetings with the other stolid, solid inhabitants of our lower middle class neighbourhood. It's soon after the war; rationing is still in force. And a man who can always lay his hand to a bit of beef for the right customer is one to be respected. My Father.

"Hiya, tyke." The iron clang of the gate is lost in the happy ring of his voice. In one swooping motion his young, strong right hand has swept me up to the scary heights of his shoulder. "Let's go and see your Mum."

Laughing, gushing the inconsequential effluvia of a child's day, I duck with practiced ease as we pass the lintel of the door. As usual, his free left hand holds a parcel of brown paper and string. It is wet. Seeping blood.

Often, as he reached out to ruffle my blond hair, passing down the long hallways of our house, or as I sat and played at his feet before the sitting-room fire on late winter afternoons, I would see in his hands cracked rivers and gullies, threads and knots of dried black blood, etching the lines of his palms; fatal lines that no amount of hand-scrubbing could totally efface.

At night, I would dream of licking them clean.

"Paul, I tell you there's something wrong with him. I mean *really* wrong. I think we're out of our depth here. He needs specialist help."

"May, for Christ's sake, are you trying to tell me that my son - our son - needs a psychiatrist? Just because he's been in a playground scrap?"

"Oh God, this wasn't just a scrap, Paul. Jonathan's

parents are considering legal action. Miss Parks said it took her and two male teachers to get Richard off him. And I saw Jonathan at the hospital, Paul. That boy might lose his *ear*!"

"Well I taught him to stand up for himself, didn't I? And wasn't that other boy bigger? And hadn't he been tormenting Richard for weeks? The way I see it, he pushed his luck once too often, and Richard pushed back. And as for the fight, well, it's easy to lose control in the heat of the moment, go a bit further than you intended..."

"That's rubbish and you know it. Yes, Jonathan had been teasing him, Miss Parks said so. But she also said he hadn't done anything today. The attack was completely unprovoked. Cold-blooded. And if she hadn't gone back after class, Jonathan would have been alone with him. God *knows* how far it would have gone..."

"You make it sound like Richard is some kind of monster..."

"Well? Isn't he? What about when he was five, and blinded Snowy?"

"An accident. He was trying to feed her, poking that stick into the hutch. A stupid kid's accident."

"And the neighbour's dog? And that cat? We almost got taken to court that time, too..."

"Alright, alright. There's no point in carrying on like this. You're upset. *I* think they were accidents; *you* don't. What does that prove? That kids are cruel? Hardly news, is it? It's a phase they go through. When I was a kid, I used to eat worms. Does that make me a psychopath? Does a fight in the playground make our son a maniac? I've spanked him and sent him to bed, and tomorrow, I'll go round and square it with Jonathan's parents. There's no real harm done, just a few stitches and one big shock. Maybe he'll pick on somebody his own size next time, eh? We'll talk to the teachers too if you like. It'll be okay, really...Now stop worrying, and c'mere..."

"You really used to eat worms? That's disgusting!"

"Yeah, and so's this..."

"Owww, Paul, stop it..."

Giggles from behind the living room door. I turn, and go back upstairs to my bedroom, thinking about Mummy. Something will have to be done...

Later. There is unspoken war between us now. She suspects that it was me who loosened the stair rods, me to blame for her broken leg. She's right.

I remember how ridiculous she looked, sprawled at the foot of the stairs; a broken doll. In unconscious- ness her skin beneath the make-up was parchment white, stretched taut, a mask. Her right leg twisted beneath her, it's new joint blooming mid-shin between knee and ankle, resplendent in its gory beauty. I remember the colours. Red-smeared white for the splintered bone, jutting jagged through the darkening, bruised purple flesh of her calf. Her stocking had torn round the break, caught perhaps on the ragged bone-edge, and had sprung back to form an irregular oval around the wound, framing the gaudy colours there in muted grey - a study in contrast, offset by the pallor of the surrounding, undamaged, flesh. Surprisingly little blood. It looked, on the whole, like a poorly-dressed leg of mutton.

I watched her for as long as I could. Eventually, as she began to stir, I let rip a carefully-rehearsed shriek of horror, and rushed into the back garden.

"Mrs.Murray, come quick. Mummy's hurt herself!"

It was, the doctor said, a bad break. Mother would never walk without a cane again. Nor, as the slowly- knitting bones robbed her of half an inch of length, without a black and clumsy cripple's boot. Yet she could say nothing to Father. What would he think of her, believing that her own young son, a mere child, had tried to kill her? Besides, in her newly-*altered* condition, Mummy was no longer as marketable a piece of merchandise as she had been before. She couldn't afford to try his patience too far. So, she hadn't died. But Mummy feared me now. And that, I learnt, was better...

It was a year of lessons. After Mother's accident, and the fight, I learned not to show my power so nakedly. Maybe it would even seem strange to call what I had power. After all, there are so many who are not willing, or able, to follow the herd of their fellows; who are, like me, alone. But of those only a few, a very few, can *choose* their loneliness; can, through simply the transformational force of their will, travel to that special place where the cattle-pen divide between the imagining of an act and its execution is abolished, and where, untethered by the suffocating charade of morality, one is *truly* free to experience the limits of sensation. From within their pens, the cattle of society can sense that power, and defer to it...Jonathan taught me this.

After the fight, whenever I met his eye, I would see fear. And daily, I would see him ridiculed for the torn and mis-shapen lump of his ear. As the weeks and months passed, I watched him diminish, marginalised, persecuted for bearing my terrible gift of mutilation. To take something shapely, and twist it; to make some- thing which moved, still. *This* was power.

For my tenth birthday, Father gave me a jack-knife. Mother shrieked, predictably.

"You can't give him that thing. He'll cut himself."

She meant: he'll cut others. Father just grinned through her protests.

"May, the boy's old enough to learn knives now. He'll be alright." I kept the blade.

And set to work with it. No ordinary knife, of course. A four inch, curving edge, hollow ground daily on my father's whetstone. The finest Swiss steel, it sliced like a lover's kiss, like a tongue of cold flame. I tempered it in the guts of rabbits trapped in snares of my own design. Not shaped or balanced for throwing, I nevertheless developed a scything throw which could bring down a bird on the wing. In two pieces. Daily, I would oil and work at its locking mechanism, until I could open it with a snap of the hand, slick as a flick-knife.

Driven by an impulse I didn't then understand, after every kill I would glide the blade into the spongy pad of my thumb, mixing my blood with that of the kill on the bare wood of the handle, rubbing both deep into the grain, until, with time and use, it assumed a dark brown, silken sheen.

In my fourteenth year, I acquired, for the first time, a popularity of sorts with my classmates. In biology class. When they would ask me to help them with the dissections they found so distasteful. Even the teacher was impressed with my professionalism as I flayed and dismembered the laboratory rats. Father was delighted.

"See," he said, "It runs in the family. He's a natural for the business, that boy."

Perhaps it was this that persuaded him. In any event, shortly afterward he arranged for me to go with him to work. To see my first official kill.

I approached the great day with all the ill-concealed excitement of a Catholic approaching confirmation; laying out my scrupulously clean "old clothes" a good three days before the event, enduring with better than usual grace Mother's tedious caveats, and on that last, sleepless night, offering up no less than three rabbits to the God of the Knife.

The morning dawned bright and clear, just as I knew it would have to. I luxuriated in the unusual pattern of it, rising an hour before my usual time (and on a schoolday, too) to share with my father his habitual breakfast of strong, near-black tea, fried eggs, and, of course, bacon. Everything seemed enhanced that day, colours brighter, sounds sharper, tastes keener. The yellow of the sun striking through the kitchen window, the red check of the table-cloth. The man-smell of my father, shaved, scrubbed pink, and enjoying his first smoke of the day. The dark, strong scent of his hand-rolling tobacco seemed to blend with the skin-stripping tannin of the tea at the back of my throat, the salt tang of the bacon on my tongue, in one almost unbearable pitch of sensation. He chose this moment to initiate me into the mystery of slaughter.

"...Now don't feel ashamed if what you see today makes you feel a bit ill. It smells a lot down there, and some of the things you're going to see aren't pretty. When your grandad took me for the first time, I was as sick as a dog, I don't mind admitting. Couldn't touch meat for a week. But you get over it. And never forget, son, that behind all that blood and guts there's an art, and a very special one at that. These people who like their bit of bacon for breakfast and a joint on Sunday - they don't want to know where it comes from, don't want to imagine what it was like when it was a whole animal, or the things that have happened to it so they can have it sitting there on the plate. So that's what they pay us for. Not just to slaughter their food for them, but to carry their guilt about it too...We're magicians, son, turning one thing into another. And artists, too. Killing can be a messy business. An ox, a cow, is a lot of weight, and just before the end, they know what's going to happen. If they can, they'll fight. I've seen a man go under the hooves of a frightened beast and come up looking like one of his own joints. So it's important to do it right. A clean kill, a quick kill. For us, and in a way, for the animals too. We owe them that at least. That dignity. Because we're in it together, the killers and the killed, against the folk who just want their Sunday roast and no worries. Our little secret. Besides..." He ended pragmatically, reaching for his coat. "Too much fear spoils the meat."

Father's was a progressive abattoir, one of the first to use humane killers; hardly out of place amongst the new neighbouring industrial units, its holding pens discreetly hidden from view. There was a lot of machinery: hoists, hooks, aerial conveyors; hoses, pumps, grilles. It looked like any production line. Only the stench, and the squealing animals, signalled its true function.

Ten were slaughtered at a time, each led into

position in narrow stalls, screened from its neighbours by corrugated iron dividers. A sling was fastened round its belly, and then tightly across its back. At this point some instinctive thrill of unease would pass through all the animals, they would begin to low frantically, and kick. Too late.

The killing began, my father passing down the line, bolt gun in hand, pausing by the head of each animal in turn. A dull report, that unearthly squealing, and on to the next. It took seconds, each carcass slumping in its sling, ready to be hoisted away, bled and gutted by gleaming silver machines and skilful hands. My father reached the end of the line, turned, and looked at me. A blob of greyish matter slid from the blunt end of the captive bolt.

"Alright, son?"

He looked at me quizzically. I nodded, white-faced.

"That's my boy." As he turned away, grinning, I fumbled through the material of my trouser pocket for my penis, pulling at its sticky head; feeling the hot gob of semen drying on my abdomen...

That was decades ago. Father is dead now, victim of one of those careless accidents he warned me against, lungs crushed between a dying bullock and the pen wall. Mother followed soon after. I think because she wanted to cheat me of the chance to arrange something myself...I live alone in the house they left me, eking out my days with these commonplace assassinations. For though I thought then that the simple thrill of execution would never pall, it has. At least in this workaday way. And so...

And so I return to the slaughterhouse by night. Pick out some beast which has about it the right quality of fear; and kill it. The old way. The good way. Feeling the recoil of it all the way up my arm as the coalhammer finds that precise, fragile point between its eyes...Eggshells in velvet. The beast sags, twitching, stunned, dying, but not yet dead, swinging in the hoist. And *then*...

Not for me the mundane perversions of the slow-eyed

labourers, caught sometimes in the cold store, cocks buried in animal cunts that are yet warmer to them than their wives. I am beyond that. And so I carve for myself new orifices for pleasure, from the animal's dying flesh. The exquisite suck of its intestine. The rubbery slip of its liver. Or, through the multiple penetrations of blade and saw, the lacerating drag of splintered ribs, along the shaft of my cock, as I fuck it in its pumping heart. Tonight, I'm going back. But soon, very soon, I shall share this new eroticism with a woman. I know where she lives, and the in- struments are prepared...

"Some kind of gangland killing? Witchcraft?"

"Beats me. Nasty, though, eh?"

The two detectives looked at the naked, frozen body again, swinging stiffly from the meathook buried deep in its shoulderblades. Fist-sized holes punctured the fleshy parts of its thighs, the buttocks, abdomen, and chest. Crammed into each, an animal's amputated penis.

Below the crushed temples, the slaughterman's eyes, mercifully, were shut. But his mouth was drawn back into a hideous grin. A rictus of fear. Or pleasure.

The other carcasses swung gently on their hooks.

Taken from "**THE BLACK BOOK**".

"RAISM"
(extracts)

James Havoc

Walpurgisnacht. A bifurcate tail striking sparks from the flint courtyard affords a flash of shrivelled black meat with yellow eyes, the hepatic tongue taking nourishment from the broth of our bowels, cruel breath daubing my cerebral canvas with the portrait of a rancid main beyond this prison of ageometric obsidian. A gigantic shark buoyed on the foaming ebb tide vomits forth a limbless navigator, who proclaims that the world is but an egg of dung enwreathed by dank worms; his contorted mouth recalls the lividity of nuns ravished by the phalliform crucifix. Callipygous, chained sirens perform, accompanied by the splayed gallop of amphibious colts necklaced in teeth of the sea. Discorporated on this beach of mineral fusion, witness the concentric violence of our hearth and household gods.

On this entropic night my faucal delights threaten to ravage the very firmament and its annihilating stars, and the crazed retort of my wolf-sisters cowers the wicked ice forests; our song ascends to the heavens on a glacial spume of albumen, configuration red as a necrophile frolics with his rigid consorts, auburn pelt alive with leeches, ulcerated dry tongue thirsting for the beestings of rectal parturition. Featureless tar babies suckle the supernumerary teat of their witch-dam, plug of coarse tissue on her plucked pubis surmounting the sulphur lips of a rotten meat chasm stitched tight with copper thread. Magick charms, chicken bones and effigies dangle from the zig-zag sutures. Imagine the wildest revelations of a nightcrawler blasted by forked lightning as he defaecates over a freshly-skinned skull; such are as nought when compared to these nocturnal tableaux. Where bile from witchcraft lips splashes the ground, the scorched earth crashes asunder to spit back the bones of sodomised infants. Trees gush exorcist lichen, poisons prevail. We breathe in, breathe out, breathe in the foetid anus aura of graveyard erotica.

Naked amid cackling oaks, venting hot pith from the devil rectum, my passage an avenue of ovens. A centaur shade slams into my bones; an eclipse has come to halt time, the cropped black meat is abroad. Catharsis, an orgasm of excrements leaves me butchered in its penumbra. The moon, replenished by tidal stasis, drinks the contents of my cranium, an exploded pumpkin. Gilles de Rais examines the touchstone newly prised from his caecum, pearl of a century-long gestation. The child of sodom, this rare nugget lends itself to the most delectable alchemy. Like a father hoarding strange eggs from the filial cucking bowl, shivering in rays of wan romance, the copromage transmutes base matter from his unravelled viscera into glistering armour fit for lunar deities. All substance is profoundly illuminated, the value of dung becomes evident even to the eye of a priest. Sculpted from mildew and carcinogenic stools, a fungoid imago of the sorcerer erupts from the gravid soil. Souls locked in a conundrum of disease, our progress is that of pirate seeds through oceanic slime curtains, we toil under a lugubrious precipitation of autoerotic ectoplasm, spectral scavengers in suppurating leather. Globes of ancient semen scatter like marbles across the flagstones of my face, raiding a pigskull orchard kiss the viscous eyes of a dog furred in flies, psetilential harbinger of the master himself on his palaquin of renal rats and living sickness.

Greetings from the torture gardens of Tiffauges, where priests and nuns are clamped in pillories of scar tissue. My face is a combustion of oyster fat and untamed leper meat, one hundred frigid winters have I sailed this main of ordure riddled with bellyworms and coprophagous lice, sucking dry the faeces salt avatar of Christ. The Master smeared in camphor, apricot pulps, absinthe and the ambrosia of anal copulation;

fingertips waxed with unguents pared from the mandibles of wasps asphixiated over charred diamonds, toying with diaphanous pearls torn from the scrotal clams of corsairs but one hour dead on the yardarm. Horsehair breeks ripple with a mushroom fleche implosion, vegetable anamorphosis, as a tribe of timberwolves run gauntlets beneath my skin, mounted on decaying mules the colour of desire. My sad metal clavicles climb helium chains lowered from the honey-coated crags of saturn, cadavers leap from urine vats at the clatter of fallen starfruit, souls out of focus urging a gut metallurgy, gold seeps from devil livers. Court hounds in warthog masks burst steaming and iridium-toothed from the belly of a stallion, the full pack spinning on hind legs drooling foetal livestock, shitting shrill maggots on a trip into the labyrinthine testes of the black meat, collective psyche fried in baby juice quintessence.

An amorphous beast of slavering offal dwells in the centre of the storm, hewing its wet pod from glaireous membrane, seething with the hiss of uric acid on bare incubus bone. Fathomless pupils coalesce like black mercury in eyes that are phantasmagoric smears deflecting a millenium of animal regeneration through blood glaciers, ruby prisms washing light over feral secluded faces; succubi that cling to chamber walls with broken claws rimed in rectal mucus, labia clotted with priapic resins, buttocks raddled by gouting ergotism, knee-length pubic hairs snaggled with rotting pig teeth. All fuck is abroad, loosed from arboreal lairs carpeted in wolfbane and mandragora, crooked crosses and purple chorion over defiled sodden graves. Possessed children drink each in cyclamen and hibiscus glades trampled by an unhallowed cortege; the killer visitation accentuates feline vestiges, purring six-nippled girls shred the tensed backs of their fathers, undead sisters desiccate brothers by the toll of the hunch-backed bell. Blaspheming man-cubs burrow into humus wombs, weaned on a milk of moons, until the hurricane signals vernal revenge.

Behold, the hog-headed god shall reign over the gibbering throng! Pay heed to the rebel priest impregnated by wild lobsters; blinded by sub-marine herpes, his mutant pincers yet osmose the venom to obviate these systems of incarceration. In such manner does the iconoclast flourish firebrands to illuminate the passageways of our most passionate and hidden desires, a limbo of crutches. The underworld of the Master is a complex contusion of genius and hate, pernicious allies forged by such a catalyst into a purgative of paranormal purity; the conjuring of an emetic vortex by supernatural vehemence, hailstorm of slewed rapier flesh hawsers disgorging phantasms of electrified ordure into the dreams of innocents. Here man is but a debased whore, suckling the pizzle of the wolf king; a slave, branded and mutilated, who must miscegenate with crustaceans, vying for survival amongst his millipede siblings. Hope is a desert of stemmed cogs, the disembodeied fury of bacilli; asphalt outposts offer nullification, a haven for corpse-eating fulmars.

The sound of liberation is the collapse of the High church, consumed in a perverse conflagration, molten idolators rendered down to basic nigredo, a protean clay whence springs the new flesh. Disciples are battened to great wheels of vitrified magma, fundaments agape to the four zephyrs; into these spiral apertures ragged mahogany stakes are driven for all eternity by raging hammers, orange catacombs resonant with a drenched meat whiplash of metal on skin and bone. Severed heads somersault over a cataract of granite stairs, living dead joust for weird spoils below on rafts crewed by simian tars, adrift on subterranean lakes of eyeballs, testicles and poison eggs. Vaulted crags echo with the milky implosion of spirits crushed at the whipping-post, mortified whisper of sepulchral collisions. The rituals of the nursery are perpetuated unto the discipline of the tomb, where the source of all incandescence is the cruel memory of abandoned lovers, an illusory, jaggered gash forever spraying incendiary jewels. Those who exist beneath this canopy are the insane children of a sickness that flowers into beatific visions fatally marred by the innate outsider, loop of sour nectars, the sorrow sceptre of perdition inset with vanquished diadems. Shooting stars exiled from convoluted nebulas, falling spikes of ghostly iridescence probe lonely lagoon floors, drums and ribs of galleons. Solitude replicates, poltergeist lepers unleashed by fallopian magnetism; romance of crucified manias.

"THE VENUS EYE"

(*To Rose McDowall*)

James Havoc

Coffinbound, Lovechild experienced the upper world by setting forth her left eye, Lucifer, on a supernatural leash. Prowling the local village and countryside, Lucifer would home in on sources of energy. Countless young lovers succumbed to his cyclopian inquisition; his favourite trip was the spiral down orgasmic spines. He could report the crackling voltage from a masturbating nun, then fly to embed himself in the hot arse of some farmgirl riding a jackanapes. At such times, Lovechild found Lucifer hard to control; senses overloaded by that unquenchable pupil, she would often have to struggle to retrieve her unrelenting spy. When she was finally back in blackness, the lid of her oblong box would suppurate with a mucal condensation, as if it were flesh and she the parasite within. Her face stank of lightning.

One sweet Autumn night, as Lucifer cruised the cobbled streets, hard beneath the gas-lamps so as to light his mistress' prison, he detected a prodigious incandescence emanating from one of the shuttered shops. At once he flew to its thatched roof, down through the rafters, and into the sparsely-furnished attic. It was instantly apparent that he had focussed upon a veritable furnace of lust. Shedward, the local butcher, was entertaining girls from the orphanage.

queen of this pubescent coven. She wears a roasted rack of lamb for a tiara, and is veiled in raw suet and ligatures. Her nude body has been painted all over with animal blood. A girdle of hearts rests over her hips, pallid aortas skirting her pelvis, and rib-bones dangle from her small, pierced nipples.

The next second, Shedward is up behind her in the saddle, pushing her forward over the wooden mane as he lifts his apron and starts to wipe his foreskin along her perineum. The suet mask snags on the horse's ear and slides off. Although the face beneath is caked in crimson, and the transmission of its image warped, Lovechild knows at once the identity of this teenage meat-mistress.

Her daughter.

The vision curdles, dissolves in burnt amber. Lovechild starts to turn in the grave, over and over again, shrieking, railing at the lid of her coffin, nails striping the mouldering satin. She can think of nothing save the sight of her traumatized child, and revenge upon Shedward, the defiler; abandoning all concentration on her errant eye. Unbound, Lucifer plunges into the orgiastic fray; from orifice to soaking orifice he flies, into teats and brains and testes, sucking up electricity like an orbital sponge.

Unbridled power loops into Lovechild's torn psyche, sworded and scorpionic, pricking as if the inside of her refulgent cranium is being needled by a thousand nomad hornets. Her fontanelles dilate with converse litanies and tirades, pan-pipes feeding back into a primitive night illumined by shifting occult pyres, ritual murder and the blazing effigies of reaper kings; gold and scarlet swastikas surmount the moon. Archaic stars invoke phantoms, chaos irradiating torn-out hearts in carmine necromantic chalices, fetishes and glittering coils, ditches brimming with magma and silver faeces, haunted ruins shimmering under fiery spurting arteries of the sky; upward cataracts of dog honey in a valley of tongues that speak ecstasy.

Little Michaela was first to the window, pointing

in awe towards the old graveyard. Following her wet finger, Shedward beheld what appeared to be a massive pyrotechnic display, or perhaps a fallen comet trail or conflagration of St.Elmo' fire, raging on the skyline. Spectral sparks endlessly criss-crossing a high, oscillating rampart of cosmic sulphur, while strips of mutinous energy lanced the atmosphere; tombstones, deep-sunken, like torched she-heads beneath this rainbow-hued inferno.

The butcher, a superstitious soul, often fancied he had seen faery lanterns dancing atop that hill. Loins piled high with lean steak, beady mind's eye pressed hard to a knot-hole in some mythic childhood fence, he would lie on the chopping-block imagining orgies of lesbian flower-dwellers: tiny, whip-cracking winged dominatrices in slugskin catsuits gyrating over grave-slabs lit up by blazing petals, while eunuch elfin held aloft trophies of carious, grown-up molars; borne on a warm wind, slivers of sad, charred melody. Tears would flow from the butcher's eyes then, mingling with the cords of drool upon his ample chins, as he gently wept in the shadow of spinning, strung-up heifers shod in shiny vinyl boots.

Yet this firestorm, surely, was evidence of even greater forces; forces that Shedward was already longing to enslave. Abandoning his girls, he rushed to the street, shouting out to arouse the slumbering village. Soon, a confused mob had assembled outside church; some marvelling at the nocturnal lights, others fearful of evil magicks. Brandishing his cleaver like a holy sceptre,Shedward assumed command, proclaiming that they were about to harness the secret power of the woods; then, counter-armed with wands of vaulting ignition, they stormed the coruscating cemetery.

Cold flames turn their breath to lilac steam, fixed like pinned starlings in a maze of chattering, radioactive crosses. Far below, the earth begins to rumble. Shedward imagines She of Tombs, jacking off the dead. Soon their cold semen will kiss the heavens, dousing the mob's brands like a blizzard of angel teeth. The earth splits open. Lovechild has risen from the grave.

Shrouded in luminous ash, wailing like quicksilver, she levitates above Shedward. Black fireworks erupt from the pores of her smoking skin, fanned by the creeping beat of pinions greased with satanic butter. Shedward cowers down, voiding his bowels on a poppy wreath; Lovechild descends. They are face to face. Her right eye transfixes him with hate; left Lucifer is reeled in from girl heaven. He slips inside Shedward's mind, drinking in electrical impulses and pissing them back out into the void.

From Lovechild's empty eyesocket a speckled wardrum drops, followed by a goosetail and a dildo oozing hot, sooty phlegm; the manifest debris of the miserable butcher's persona. Ant-covered dials on cords tumble out, then pork-bone pariahs, a dog in a cow's orbit, eight-balls in egg-shells, clawdust, caves within kitty, figments from a chapel of flawed diamond skulls, two clockwork sailors, thunder on hooks, skin bells cut from the boiled slaves of birds, red honey in a head-cage, keyholes, hexed cobalt breasts, a dreamboat of rats, cups of puce tears beneath a tinsel tree, and a hymenopterous cupid caul with orchids; littering the boneyard like flaccid, discarded toys in a neon nursery.

Avenged, Lovechild lapsed into putrefaction. It was the end of Shedward; all his hair fell out, and he spoke only gibberish from that day on.

Taken from "SATANSKIN".

"TWIN STUMPS"

James Havoc

Silence - sweet harbinger of disfigurement!

The family must die, but without the family there can be no sacred crimes. How mundane it is to kill or rape a mere stranger - masturbation by a ringless hand. Henry sinks his rigid kin into frosty meat pits, an ancestral burial womb insulated with sleek maternal pelts. When the full moon rises, he and the lonely dead come out to play.

Henry, last of the bloodline, presides in this organic mausoleum, where a clock driven by thorny hearts records thirteen fathoms of midnight. All the furnishings are styled from the dead. The exterior walls are proofed in human skin, tattooed with pornographic tableaux, and the roof is cobbled with eyeballs so that all the pretty stars have mirrors.

Inside, the family are at table. At the head sits Henry, and opposite him his exalted brother Griezell, a gothic foetus on nails. On either side, four generations. Mummified, necklaced in teeth and testicles, pierced all over with tarsals; some skinned at death, others at birth. Half-eaten, bladdery and bloodless, some barnacled with transplanted nipples, some sporting multiple genitalia, legs screwed into arm sockets or heads crammed inside gutted bellies. Carpal chains leak from desiccated fundaments, rare maggots squirm in brain pans and pubic wigs.

As an adolescent, Henry had visions. Gazing up nightly at the steamy firmament, he came to realise that each star above was immaculate, a perfect and uncompromised entity. Evolving from dust, and later reverting to nuclear ash, the stars had no need to marry or multiply, no need to align themselves to familial groups. Astrology was akin to vampirism; constellations arbitrary, an atavistic conceit of man.

Filthy, uncomprehending man. Groping in misery;

forever reproducing in the vain hope of burying his unutterable solitude in numbers. Slowly, his profane inter-breeding was dissipating the irradiance of his autonomous stellar analogues. Soon, the heavens would be extinguished. Henry could see but one solution: a glorious extermination of the human family.

Mocking the antics of his parents, he took to fornicating with the sows in the barn. Some grew gravid. One night a storm came, and the sows dispersed in terror, leaving behind their stillborn farrows. In the fulminating light, the tiny corpses seemed to Henry half-human. Heeding this omen, he took up the hatchet. Parents, brothers, sisters, aunts and uncles, sons and daughters alike were systematically axed and buggered, partially devoured and then preserved in subterranean vaults. The swampland acquiesced glee-fully, guarding the scene of the crime with a rampart of grasses, prickling nettles and vines, quicksands and the mauve whorls of its erotic trees, whilst providing a fodder of dwarf hogs, mambas, and hot, horny fruits.

Every full moon, Henry re-enacts his violations.

Tonight, there must be a trial. Henry has reason to believe that Uncle Nexus, spurred by renegade shafts of sunlight, has slithered in his tomb and committed acts upon Mother, impregnating her with lobster claws and the jawbone of an ass. Soon, she may give birth to reeking shells or albino centaurs, crippled with eyes of syphilis resin; venomous usurpers in the mortuary.

Henry brings order with three sharp raps of his shinbone gavil. He turns to address the jury, thirteen puppets of addled blubber roped in a spinal gallery. Just then, the skies occlude with an inflorescence of whippoorwills; a lilting, disembodied voice interrupts proceedings, soiling the chapter of his law.

It comes from without. Pale Henry quits the chamber to locate its source. In his head, a mess of sick talons, itching; his breath like a premature burial. Trembling, he is lured into the gloom by a nursery lament, its chasmal sadness spelling the assassination of liberty. A girl child is sitting cross-legged in front of a skull-ringed acacia, scraping shit from her shoes as she sings; a stain on her panties recalling the genesis of comets. Confusion. This girl is not of the family. What possible fun then in stringing her up, whether it be to butcher or sodomise? Yet here she is, fresh from the marsh, an outsider in the gnarls.

She has a sticky doll with her, a tar baby dappled with hornets and dragonflies, and she calls it Miss Leopard. Miss Leopard has guided them through the swamp; now she tugs her companion to her feet. The two visitors start to skip in circles, widdershins, the little girl singing a heart-rending ode to ravens. Entranced, Henry flings himself to the ground, face pressed close to the rank loam, contorted as if licking dog-meat from a soft trap. His exterminating angel has descended.

Snakes pass. Girl and tar baby veer off into the swamp. Henry hurries after, powerless to combat his inexplicable attraction to the intruder; his every fibre ablaze with an insurgent desire to maim, to crush, to crucify.

Ablaze with love.

Deeper and deeper into the humid vegetation he pursues them, through vast spider-webs decorated with mortal remains, pools of iridescent vermin, leeches on the wing. Too late, he realises they have entered the quicksands.

Their trail is obscure. Henry hesitates. On the point of turning back, he sees the girl appear across a tarn, waving her panties like voodoo. Sure of his attention, she hitches up her dress, legs apart, giggling as she displays her hairless loins, tattooed with pig skulls, before skittering off. With a bellow of lust Henry lurches after her, mindful only of a crimson slit amid the ink-bones; yearning to snap the pinions of desire between his ceremonial fingers. His thoughts are sparks vaulting through the blackest pit. Within his soul, the geometry of molten lard.

In a trice, the thirsty sands envelop him.

The girl reappears. She raises her skirts again, this time twisting to display her small buttocks. There, at the root of her spine, hangs a stubby, curled pink tail. She defaecates loudly, her excreta resembling clusters of steaming raisins, then kicks off her shoes, aiming at the drowning man's head, to reveal a pair of ragged trotters. With that, she vanishes, giggling, hand in hand with tar baby. Spewing grit and slime, Henry perceives that his teenage nebula has regrouped; a spectre of high holy incest is once more roosting in the mangroves.

The moon wanes. From the vitrified sky, winter photons that kiss with thin cyanose lips, charged with universal melancholy. The swamp folds in on itself; the quicksands swallow the last of Henry. In his crypt, the family still sits, motionless, at the mercy of the disintegrating dawn. Their last living descendant is playing with Miss Leopard among the flytraps.

Taken from "SATANSKIN".

"BODY BAG"
(*extracts*)

Henry Rollins.

HE WAS EVERYTHING YOU COULD WANT IN A CHILD KILLER. HE LIVED ALONE. HE SENT LETTERS TO HIS MOM EVERY DAY, TELLING HER EXACTLY WHAT HE HAD DONE AND WANT HE WANTED TO DO. HE PUT THE LETTERS IN AN ENVELOPE AND ADDRESSED IT "MOM, HEAVEN". HE MASTURBATED IN THE DARK, HE PICKED CRAB LICE FROM HIS SCROTUM AND BURST THEM BETWEEN HIS FRONT TEETH. WELL, HE HAD DONE IT, FOUR TIMES TOTAL, THREE IN ONE SUMMER, ONE BOY THREE GIRLS. THE BOY HAD BEEN FIRST, A DESTITUTE WOMAN HAD FOUND THE BODY IN A DUMPSTER WHILE SEARCHING FOR FOOD. THE BOY'S PENIS AND TESTICLES HAD BEEN REMOVED AS WELL AS THE TONGUE AND EYES. THE POLICE DETECTIVES NEVER FOUND THEM AND WHY WOULD THEY? THEY WERE AT HOME IN THE FREEZER. THE GIRLS WERE FOUND IN ASSORTED PLACES, AND MUTILATED IN VARIOUS WAYS. THERE WERE SIMILARITIES HOWEVER, THE EYES, TONGUE AND NIPPLES HAD BEEN REMOVED FROM ALL THREE; ONE, THE THIRTEEN YEAR OLD, HAD REALLY TURNED HEADS AT THE CITY MORGUE. HE HAD TAKEN AN EMPTY MALT LIQUOR BOTTLE AND INSERTED IT SO FAR INTO HER VAGINA THAT THE NECK WAS DEEPLY LODGED IN HER LIVER. THE CORONERS REASONED THAT THE ONLY WAY HE COULD HAVE POSSIBLY DONE IT WAS TO HAVE GRABBED THE GIRL BY THE ANKLES AND TO HAVE INSERTED IT WITH HIS FOOT. WHATEVER, THE SUMMER WAS YOUNG AND HE WAS GETTING RESTLESS AND LONELY AGAIN.

...

I SIT IN A DIFFERENT JAIL HOUSE. I WRAP MY FINGERS AROUND MY JAILCELL EYES AND BEAT MY TIN CUP AGAINST MY RIBS. SOMEONE LEFT THE GATE TO THE FIELDS OF HUMANITY OPEN. ONE NIGHT I CREPT IN, WITH A JAIL HOUSE MIND, WITH A THOUGHT, WITH A WISH, AND I SLAUGHTERED THE FIELDS, I BURNED THEM TO THE GROUND.

LOOK AT THE PEOPLE DANCING IN THE FIELDS.

HUMAN HARVEST.
I WATCH ALL OF THOSE IN ATTENDENCE. THRU SCARECROW EYES THE FIELDS ARE ON FIRE, AND EVERYBODY'S BURNING. PILES OF LOVERS, STACKED IN TWISTED HEAPS, DOUSED WITH GASOLINE AND SET TO BURN. PILES OF DEAD BODIES BURNING. I LISTEN TO THE OIL CRACKLE OF SMOULDERING HAIR AND FLESH. I'M STILL ALIVE. I AM TOO EMPTY TO BURN. WHEN I CLOSE MY EYES I CAN STILL HEAR THEIR SCREAMS. I REMEMBER THEIR LAST DANCE, BEFORE I LIT THE FIELDS AFLAME. IT WAS BEAUTIFUL.

...

I DON'T THINK THAT THIS ROAD WILL EVER END. SOMETIMES I GET SO TIRED THAT I THINK I WILL FALL OFF. I HAVE LOOKED HIGH AND LOW AND I CAN'T FIND ANYONE ELSE HERE. THE NIGHTS ARE SO COLD THAT I CAN'T SEEM TO EVER WARM UP. I HAVE BEEN OUT HERE FOR AWHILE AND I WILL PROBABLY BE OUT HERE FOREVER. I CAN TELL, THIS ROAD HATES ME, THIS ROAD DOES NOT WANT ME HERE. I DON'T KNOW WHERE ELSE TO GO. SOMETIMES I GET SO LONELY THAT I THINK I'M GONNA BREAK IN PIECES, LIKE BROKEN GLASS, LIKE A BOTTLE DROPPED ONTO PAVEMENT, ALL BROKE UP.

THERE WAS A CAR CRASH, A POWERFUL CAR CRASH. HEAPS OF TWISTED MUSCLE MACHINE. THE ENGINE DIED SCREAMING, WRAPPED ITS TEETH AROUND A TREE. IN THE BOWELS OF THE WRECK WAS A GIRL. THE MOST BEAUTIFUL GIRL I HAD EVER SEEN. THE CRASH HAD BEEN ABRUPT, CRUDE. BUT EVEN THIS COULD NOT MAR HER. BROKEN GLASS MADE A GLITTERING NECKLACE AROUND HER NECK. HER HEAD WAS CRUDELY THROWN BACK, SPLAYING BEAUTIFUL CHESTNUT-BROWN HAIR AROUND HER SHOULDERS AND FACE. HER EYES WERE WIDE OPEN AND STARING OUT. IT'S HARD FOR ME TO EXPLAIN WHAT HER EYES WERE SAYING, THEY HAD A LOOK OF WISE INNOCENCE, OF JADED VIRGINITY, I'LL NEVER FORGET HER EYES. HER FACE WAS COMPOSED, BEAUTIFUL, SAINT-LIKE. HER LEGS WERE RUDELY SPREAD AND BROKEN AS IF THE CAR HAD RAPED HER BEFORE I HAD GOTTEN THERE. ONE HAND RESTED ON HER THIGH AS IF TO PROTECT HERSELF FROM ATTACK AND THE

OTHER WAS THROWN BACK OVER THE HEADREST WITH SUBMISSIVE ABANDON. THE NIGHT AIR WAS FULL OF HER PERFUME.
I NEVER SAW HER ALIVE, SHE NEVER LIED TO ME ONCE.

...

DADDY, YOU ARE IN YOUR BED ASLEEP. YOUR WIFE IS LYING NEXT TO YOU. SHE IS YOURS, YOUR WOMAN. SHE'S YOURS. I HAVE COME TO YOUR HOUSE. IN YOUR SLEEP YOU FEEL A SHARP PAIN IN YOUR HEAD. I HAVE JUST SLAPPED YOU. YOU ARE AWAKE, YOUR EYES WIDEN IN FEAR, IT'S DARK, YOU DON'T RECOGNIZE ME, OUR EYES MEET. I'M LOOKING IN YOU, THRU YOU MY EYES ARE LIKE TWO BULLETS RIPPING THROUGH YOUR FACE. THE TABLES HAVE TURNED, IT'S GOOD NOW, YOUR WIFE HAS TURNED INTO A MASS OF PUTRID BLACK TAR AND IS OOZING OFF THE BED. I HAVE MUSCLES, THEY ARE STRONG, I CAN UTILIZE CRUSHING POWER. YOU ARE OLDER, WEAK, YOUR BONES ARE BRITTLE, YOU ARE COMPLETELY DEFENCELESS, I KNOW THIS AND FULLY TAKE ADVANTAGE OF IT. YOUR MOUTH IS OPEN, YOUR JAW IS WORKING, YOU ARE MAKING FAINT RASPING SOUNDS, BUT NO WORDS COME FROM YOUR MOUTH. GET UP! GET UP! I TOLD YOU TO GET UP AND YOU DO. NOW, SAY MY NAME, TELL ME WHO I AM, YOU SAY NOTHING, YOU ARE MAKING SLIGHT CHOKING SOUNDS, WHAT'S MY NAME, WHO AM I? DO YOU REMEMBER ME? I AM 2-13-61, I AM 2-13-61. MY LEFT FIST COMES STRAIGHT AT YOU, YOU SEE IT IN SLOW MOTION, YOUR FACE EXPLODES LIKE A PANE OF GLASS, SOMETHING BROKE, YOUR RIGHT CHEEK IS CRUSHING COMPLETELY. YOU WOULD FALL TO THE GROUND IF I DID NOT HAVE A HOLD OF YOUR TRACHEA, I'M NOT EVEN SWEATING, YOU ARE OLD AND WEAK, IT'S SIMILAR TO BEATING A CHILD. YOU REMEMBER NOW. YOU ARE SEEING BRIGHT BLUE FLASHES AND SPOTS IN YOUR EYES, I AM SQUEEZING YOUR TRACHEA SHUT, THE CARTILAGE MAKES A RUBBERY SNAP-CRACK-POP AS I CRUSH IT. I NOW START SHAKING YOU BY IT. YOUR FEET ARE OFF THE GROUND, THEY DANGLE AS I SHAKE YOU
HEY DAD
HEY DAD
I LEARNED

I LEARNED RESPECT
I LEARNED DISCIPLINE
I HAVE STRENGTH
YOUR EYES ARE RIVETED TO THE CEILING
YOU SEE 2-13-61
CLEARLY
PERFECTLY
LIKE A CHILD.

...

IN THE DARK UNMOVING STILL OF THE NIGHT
TWO LOVERS
THEIR BODIES TWIST AND COIL
LIKE LOOPS
ON A HANGMAN'S NOOSE.
AS THE SUN APPROACHES
THEY SHRINK AND SEPARATE
AND SPEAK IN HUMAN TONES
DEATH TRIP
IN HERE
RIGHT NOW.

...

I WAS IN THIS APARTMENT IN THE EAST VILLAGE. I SAW THIS GUY SHOOTING UP HEROIN. HE TIED OFF HIS LEFT ARM WITH AN EXTENSION CORD. HE PUT THE NEEDLE IN HIS ARM. THE BLOOD WENT UP THROUGH THE NEEDLE AND MIXED WITH THE HEROIN. HE HAD HIT THE VEIN. HE SHOT THE HEROIN AND BLOOD MIXTURE INTO HIS ARM. HE RELEASED THE EXTENSION CORD AND PULLED OUT THE NEEDLE. HE BENT FORWARD AND VOMITED ALL OVER HIS LAP. HE LEANED BACK AGAINST THE WALL. A TRAIL OF SPITTLE CAME FROM HIS MOUTH ONTO HIS SHIRT. HIS ARM WAS BLEEDING, I NOTICED BLACK AND BLUE BRUISES FROM WHERE THERE WERE PREVIOUS NEEDLE PUNCTURES. HE DIDN'T BOTHER TO WIPE UP THE BLOOD, VOMIT OR SPITTLE, HE SEEMED UNCONCERNED. HE SEEMED HAPPY. I DON'T KNOW, SEEMED KINDA NICE.

WATCHING THIS DUDE SHOOT UP: I LIKE STICKING NEEDLES IN MY ARM. EVERY TIME I DO, I GET HIGH, I FEEL GOOD,

I SAY FUCK YOU. WHEN I THROW UP I THROW UP ON YOU. WHEN I NOD OUT, I NOD OUT ON YOU AND YOUR FUCKED-UP WORLD. THE TRACKS ON MY ARMS ARE ALL THE TIMES I WON, ALL THE TIMES I SAID FUCK YOU. I LIKE STICKING NEEDLES IN MY ARM! I DO SO MUCH STICKING THAT I DON'T EVEN THINK OF STICKING IT IN. YOU KNOW, I DON'T GET HARD. I DON'T NEED NO FUCKING BITCH TO FUCK WITH ME. NO GIRL CAN MAKE ME FEEL LIKE THIS. I LIKE STICKING NEEDLES IN MY ARM!

...

I WAS RUNNING ON THE STRAND DOWN NEAR THE HERMOSA BEACH PIER. IT WAS A CLEAR DAY. EVERYBODY WAS OUTSIDE. I SAW ALL THESE PEOPLE IN SHORTS AND BIKINIS, HAVING BEERS, PLAYING VOLLEYBALL ON THE SAND, RUNNING AROUND, LAUGHING, CALLING OUT TO EACH OTHER, COOKING HAMBURGERS ON HIBACHIS, PLAYING ZZ TOP, FOOLING AROUND ON SKATEBOARDS, BEAUTIFUL GIRLS, ALL TANNED AND SLIM, SMILING AND TALKING WITH GUYS, PEOPLE GETTING DRUNK - TALKING LOUD AND LAUGHING LIKE A BUNCH OF HYENAS - MIGHT HAVE BEEN NICE TO HAVE BEEN PART OF IT.

I SAW THIS GUY WALKING DOWN THE STREET WITH THIS GIRL. THEY WERE BOTH SMILING, THEY WERE HOLDING HANDS. YOU KNOW SHE WAS ONE OF THOSE BLONDES, AND SHE HAD ON THESE NICE CLOTHES, AND THEY WERE LAUGHING AND TALKING JUST WALKING DOWN THE STREET, PROBABLY GOING TO EAT DINNER AND THEN GO TO A MOVIE OR A PLAY...I WOULD HAVE TRADED PLACES WITH THE GUY IN A SECOND.

...

WHEN I SEE THE GIRLS WALKING DOWN THE STREET I WANT TO FUCK, I GET TO FEELING CRAZY. I WANT TO BREED, I WANT TO EAT A MILE OF PUSSY. OUT OF MY HEAD.

...

I AM THE INCINERATION MAN. A DISCIPLE OF THE SUN. I'M YOUR MAN. I DON'T WANT TO WASTE YOUR TIME. I DON'T WANT TO TAKE YOU ANYWHERE, I WANT TO TAKE YOU

NOWHERE. I'VE GOT A MAGIC TORCH. BLOW OUT THE CANDLES ON YOUR BIRTHDAY CAKE, GET IN THE CAR, WE ARE GONNA FLAME BROTHER.

IN BEAUTIFUL REDONDO BEACH ON ARTESIA BLVD. RIGHT NEAR THAT 7-11. THAT'S WHERE THE PINKHOUSE LIVES. CHEAP SHIT PLASTER, LAUGHING CAR SALESMEN, SHADE TREES. THE NIGHTS ARE HOT AND FULL. NO ONE WILL HEAR YOUR SCREAMS WHEN YOU ARE SLAUGHTERED IN THE BACK ROOMS OF THE FILTHY PINKHOUSE.

ANCIENT INDIAN TRIBES IN CENTRAL AMERICA USED TO HAVE HUMAN SACRIFICES. THE HIGH PRIESTS WOULD CUT OUT THE HEART OF THE SACRIFICED AND EAT IT. THEY WOULD PROBABLY CALL US PRIMITIVE AND VIOLENT FOR THE WAY WE LIVE TODAY. I WOULD HAVE TO AGREE.

...

I SAW A COLOR PICTURE OF A BLACK MAN HANGING BY HIS NECK. THE PICTURE WAS NOT OLD. HE WAS DRESSED LIKE YOU OR I MIGHT DRESS. IT WAS SAID TO BE A K.K.K. KILLING. THERE WAS THIS BLACK DUDE SWINGING FROM A ROPE THAT WAS TIED TO A TREE BRANCH. I BELIEVE IN WHEELS, LIKE WHAT GOES AROUND COMES AROUND AND ALL THAT. I WONDER WHAT THE HANGPERSON OR HANGPERSONS HEAR AT NIGHT. THAT IS A MIGHTY WHEEL, A CRUSHING WHEEL. I WONDER IF THE HANGPERSON OR HANGPERSONS EVER HEAR THE ROAR OF THEIR WHEEL, ROLLING DOWN THE TRAIL. I AM TALKING ABOUT THE ROAR OF THE WHEEL.

...

A BUM STOOD AT THE LUCKY MARKET RIGHT IN FRONT OF ARTESIA & BLOSSOM. HE WAS BEGGING FOR MONEY. HE LOOKED PRETTY PATHETIC, DRESSED IN RANCID, OILY CLOTHES. HE SMELLED LIKE CIGARETTES AND URINE. "CAN YOU SPARE A DIME?" HE WOULD ASK. PEOPLE WOULD SHAKE THEIR HEADS OR WALK WAY ROUND HIM. HE WAS GETTING NOWHERE. TWO HOURS WENT BY, NO MONEY, NOT A CENT. "PLEASE, A DIME!" CRIED THE BUM. A MIDDLE-AGED MAN WALKED BY HIM, HEARD HIS PLEA AND LAID UPON HIM A

MINT NEW DIME FROM HIS PANTS POCKETS. "THANK YOU, SIR! THANK YOU!" SHOUTED THE BUM. DIME IN HAND, THE BUM LIMPED OVER TO A PHONE BOOTH AND CALLED IN THE AIR STRIKE.

...

WHEN WE ARE LYING NEXT TO EACH OTHER, I LOOK AT HER NAKED BODY. I TRY TO IMAGINE SOMEONE ELSE ENTERING HER, KISSING HER. I TRY BUT I CAN'T, I CAN, BUT I CAN'T REALLY.

...

I SAW GOD
WHILE I WAS FUCKING YOUR MOTHER
I SAW GOD
WHILE I WAS MAKING YOUR WIFE SUCK MY COCK
I SAW GOD WHILE I WAS KILLING YOUR KIDS
I SAW GOD IN THE LUCKY MARKET
DIRTY - GREASY
KILLER
KILLER
LOVER
LOVER
GOD SMILES DOWN ON ME
HE MAKES THE SUN SHINE FOR ME
I'VE SEEN GOD
YOU HAVEN'T
I SAW GOD
WHILE I WAS CHOKING YOU
—HE WAS SMILING.

...

OH BABY
YOU GOTTA BE GOOD TO YOUR MAN.
HE WORKS SO HARD FOR YOU BABY
HE WANTS TO BE A GOOD DOG FOR YOU BABY
HE WANTS TO CALL YOU BABY, MOMMA
YOU GOTTA PLEASE YOUR MAN
TAKE HIM BY THE HAND
LOOK INTO HIS EYES

TAKE HIM INTO THE BEDROOM
LAY HIM DOWN
LAY HIM DOWN
TURN OFF THE LIGHTS
MAKE HIM FEEL GOOD
MAKE HIM FEEL GOOD
YOU KNOW HOW
USE YOUR MOUTH
MAKE HIM FEEL GOOD
LISTEN TO HIS BREATHING
IN OUT
IN OUT
YEAH, HE'S BREATHING HARD
HE'S CALLING YOU BABY
REACH UNDER THE PILLOW
PULL OUT THE KNIFE
CUT
IT
OFF
THE WHOLE THING
CUT IT OFF
LISTEN TO HIM SCREAM
LISTEN TO HIM SCREAM
GO TO THE KITCHEN
WASH YOUR MOUTH OUT
MEN ARE PIGS
YES
MEN ARE PIGS
PUT IT IN AN ENVELOPE
SEND IT TO ME
DO IT
TONIGHT
CUT IT OFF
RIP IT OUT
MEN ARE PIGS
SEND IT TO ME
NO ONE UNDERSTANDS YOU
LIKE I DO

...

WHEN I LOOK INTO HER EYES
I SEE
A FIRE BURNING
NOT THE FIRE OF DESIRE
NOT THE FIRE OF LOVE
THE FIRE OF DEAD BODIES
PILED IN MOUNDS
THE FIRE OF PLAGUE AND PESTILENCE
SHE IS NAPALM
BURNED TO DEATH BY NAPALM
HAVE YOU SEEN THEM RUNNING,
SCREAMING,
FLESH BURNING, CURLING BACK
MY LOVE FOR HER
IS A CRAWLING FAMINE
CLAWING AT HER SOUL
SHE BURNS WITH NAPALM
I CRAVE HER DESTRUCTION
SHE LIGHTS UP THE JUNGLE
SHE BURNS
WITH NAPALM

...

I DRILLED A HOLE INTO THE BACK OF MY HEAD. IT WAS EASY. I TOOK A BLACK & DECKER POWER DRILL AND PUT IT TO MY HEAD. THE DRILL BIT CHEWED THROUGH MY SCALP, NO PROBLEM, A LITTLE BIT OF SMOKE CAME UP WHEN THE BIT HIT MY SKULL. I GAVE IT A GOOD PUSH AND IT CRUNCHED THRU TO MY BRAIN. I STUFFED A BIT OF PAPER TOWEL IN THE HOLE, NOW, WHEN THE PRESSURE GETS TO BE TOO MUCH, I PULL OUT THE CORK AND LET MY BRAINS DRAIN OUT SOME. A LITTLE BIT OF STICKY JUICE COMES OUT. THE PRESSURE'S OFF. IF YOU WANT TO GET RID OF PROBLEMS, GET RID OF THEM.

...

WHEN YOU TAKE A YOUNG CHILD INTO THE BACK YARD. WHEN YOU SNAP ITS SPINE WITH YOUR HANDS, WHEN YOU DECAPITATE THE CORPSE, WHEN YOU CUT OPEN ITS STOMACH AND CLEAN OUT THE STEAMING ENTRAILS INTO A BUCKET,

WHEN YOU INSERT A SKEWER THRU THE ANUS THAT EXITS THRU THE NECK-STUMP, WHEN YOU TIE THE LITTLE HANDS AND ARMS BACK, WHEN YOU PUT THE CORPSE OVER THE COALS AND START TO TURN IT, AROUND AND AROUND, WHEN THE SKIN IS CHARRED BLACK AND JUICE IS DRIPPING OFF THE CORPSE ONTO THE HISSING COALS, IT DOESN'T EVEN LOOK HUMAN ANYMORE. NOT HUMAN. ANYMORE.

...

COCKROACHES ARE YOUR GODS. YOU ARE WEAK. YOU SHOULD PRAY TO THEM. THEY ARE A MORE PERFECT LIFE FORM THAN YOU. YOU ARE FUCKED UP, WITH YOUR IDIOTIC IDIOSYNCRASIES. YOU HAVE ANALYSTS, TRANQUILIZERS, YOU NEED VACATIONS, YOU START WARS, YOU COMMIT SUICIDE, YOU STEAL, YOU LIE, YOU CHEAT. YOU ARE WEAK. YOU CANNOT SURVIVE, YOU ARE TOO BUSY HAULING AROUND THAT BIG BRAIN OF YOURS, YOU HAVE TO BUILD JAILS TO KEEP YOUR KIND FROM KILLING YOU! YOU KILL EVERYTHING. YOU LIVE IN FEAR. YOU COULD NEVER LIVE WITH THE SIMPLICITY AND BEAUTY OF THE 'ROACH. YOU HAVE ABORTIONS. YOU ENGAGE IN MEANINGLESS ACTIVITY. YOU ARE WEAK, COCKROACHES ARE YOUR GODS. YOU ARE NOT EVEN FIT TO KISS THE SMOOTH BELLY SCALES OF THE MOTHER 'ROACH, YOU ARE REPULSED BY THEM, YOU FEAR THEM. THERE ARE MORE OF THEM THAN THERE ARE OF YOU, YOU GET SQUEAMISH AT JUST THE SIGHT, THEY MAKE YOU SICK. YOU ARE WEAK. COCKROACHES ARE YOUR GODS, GIVE UP YOUR PLATE OF FOOD TO THEM, WHETHER YOU DO OR NOT, THEY WILL SURVIVE YOU AND YOUR STUPIDITY. YOU TRY TO KILL THEM WITH GAS AND POISON JUST LIKE YOU DO TO YOUR OWN KIND, THE 'ROACH COMES BACK, STRONGER, FASTER, MORE IMMUNE. YOU WATCH TELEVISION, YOU LOCK YOUR DOORS TO PROTECT YOURSELF FROM YOUR RACE. YOU PUT NEEDLES IN YOUR ARMS, YOU SELL YOUR BODIES, YOU FIND NEW AND INVENTIVE WAYS TO MUTILATE YOURSELVES AND OTHERS. YOU ARE WEAK. COCKROACHES ARE YOUR GODS.

...

"DEATH SONG"

Henry Rollins

I STAND AT MY WINDOW AND LISTEN.
I HEAR THE SIRENS.
ONE AFTER ANOTHER AS THEY WAIL BY.
SIRENS GUNSHOTS AND HELICOPTERS.
ALL THE TIME IN THIS NEIGHBOURHOOD.
I AM LUCKY.
I LIVE IN A GOOD ONE.
THE BEAST HAS BEEN WOUNDED.
IT CRASHES THRU THE UNDERBRUSH,
ROARING AND SNORTING.
THE BEAST IS SO HEAVY,
AND HAS BEEN RUNNING FOR SO LONG,
THAT IT WILL TAKE YEARS FOR IT TO FALL.
MEANWHILE WE WAIT.
IN ALL KINDS OF SPACES.
WATCHING TELEVISION.
MARVELING AT THE CRIMINALS.
THE ONES THAT HAVE THE MOST CHARISMA,
ARE THE ONES THAT WE ROOT FOR.
GLAD IT WASN'T US.
THE BEAST IS HOWLING TONIGHT.
TRYING TO PULL THE SHRAPNEL FROM ITS JOINTS.
IT'S COMING TO BLOOD AND RUST.
BLOOD AND RUST.
THAT'S ALL THAT WILL BE FOUND OF ME,
WHEN THEY COME TO SEE WHY I DIDN'T PAY THE RENT.
THEY WILL SAY:
YEAH, HE WAS PART ANIMAL, PART MACHINE,
BUT THAT WASN'T ENOUGH.
TELL WHATS-HER-NAME TO GET IN HERE AND CLEAN THIS UP.
TO MAKE IT THRU THE DEATH SONG,
THE RIGHT STONE THROW.
THE RIGHT DANCE THRU THE MINEFIELD.
IT'S ALL IN THE WALK.
AND HOW YOU STAND UP
TO INTIMIDATION, HUMILIATION AND VIOLENCE.

THE BEAST IS SHUDDERING AT MY BLUES SONG.
SHOWING ITS TEETH.
1000 SUICIDE GLORY THOUGHTS LATER,
AND I'M STILL HERE,
IT'S STILL HERE.
THE CARS ARE CRASHING TONIGHT.
BLOOD AND RUST.
THE LAST FEW NIGHTS
THERE HAVE BEEN GUNSHOTS ACROSS THE STREET.
THE FACT THAT THE POLICE NEVER COME,
DOESN'T MEAN A DAMN THING.
YOU SEE WHAT I MEAN?
LAST WEEK I WAS IN THE MID-WEST.
OMAHA, NEBRASKA.
THERE WAS REAL RAIN.
HEAT LIGHTNING.
THE SKY WAS SWELLING.
ELECTRIC SNAKES COILED AND STRUCK.
DARTING IN AND OUT OF WARRIOR CLOUDS,
THEY LOOKED AS IF THEY WERE GOING TO EXPLODE.
I ASKED SOMEONE
IF THIS WOULD BE A GOOD PLACE TO MOVE TO.
HE SAID NO.
I ASKED WHY NOT.
HE TOLD ME THAT NOTHING EVER HAPPENS HERE.
IT'S A HOLLOW FACELESS SONG
THAT THIS PLACE LEAVES YOU SINGING.
ALL ALONE TO YOURSELF.
AS YOU CLAP SPOONS ON THE KITCHEN SINK,
TO KEEP TIME WITH THE CRIME.
HEY THAT RHYMES.
AS CRIME GOES BY.
AS I SIT IN A DOORWAY, THINKING.
THIS GIRL TOLD ME THAT SHE WANTED TO JOIN THE CIRCUS.
A REAL CIRCUS.
I ASKED HER SINCE WHEN IS THE ONE
ON HOLLYWOOD BLVD. NOT GOOD ENOUGH?
SHE DIDN'T THINK I WAS FUNNY AT ALL.

Taken from "THE JACKASS THEORY".

"GOLDENBOY"
Henry Rollins

HOW DO YOU LIKE THE NEW GOLDEN BOY?
MAGIC PARASITE.
ON THE CORNER.
MADE TO ORDER.
SOON TO DIE.
SUCKING. SUCKING. SUCKING.
1-2-3-4
CRIMINAL ARISE.
LICK THE ASHES FROM THE WOUNDS.
LICK THE BLOOD FROM THE MOUTHS.
SMACK YOUR LIPS.
PACK YOUR PIECE.
HIT THE STREETS.
REAL ROCK AND ROLL.
GET UP EARLY.
THERE'S A LOT OF NEW FLESH
TO MUTILATE.
THE FIELDS OF BODIES.
LOST SELFLESS,
SLAUGHTERED DAILY.
YOU CAN DO SO MUCH
WHEN YOU'RE STUPID.
WHEN YOU TRUST.
WHEN YOU OPEN WIDE.
AND SAY, I DO.
BACK TO THE GOLDEN PARASITE.
LOVE AFFAIR WITH MILLIONS.
BLOOD LETTING IN THE HOME.
AMAZING WHAT YOU CAN DO
WHEN YOU PUT YOUR MIND TO IT.
TERRIFYING WHAT YOU WILL DO
WHEN YOU CAN'T CONTROL IT.
DAY AFTER DAY.
PAYING SICK HOMAGE TO THE GOD.
THE GOLDEN PARASITE.
WALKING ON COALS.

DOING 1001 DANCES.
EXPENDING,
FIGHTING OFF THE URGE
TO END IT ALL.
DIDN'T YOU KNOW
IT'S ALREADY OVER.
THAT'S HOW IT GOES WITH THE PARASITE.
THE GOLDEN SUCKER.
THE SEXY MIND FUCK.
DEATH'S CHEERLEADER.
THAT'S OUR BOY.
I KEEP WAITING FOR YOU TO DROP.
I KEEP THINKING THAT
I'M GOING TO READ ABOUT YOU
AND HOW YOU FELL.
BUT IT NEVER HAPPENS.
I DON'T KNOW WHERE IT ALL CAME FROM.
I WANT YOU TO TELL YOU ABOUT A MAN.
A REAL MAN.
I WATCHED HIM
SWEAT BLEED AND SCREAM
THRU HOT LIT NIGHTS
OF BRUTAL HUMAN TESTS.
SOMETIMES I THOUGHT
HE WAS GOING TO EXPLODE
OR BURST INTO FLAME.
HE SCARED ME.
INSPIRED ME.
PUSHED ME UPWARDS AND ONWARDS.
LIKE IS THERE ANY OTHER WAY TO GO?
I WATCHED HIM DIE.
I SAW IT HAPPEN RIGHT IN FRONT OF ME.
HE GAVE UP.
CURLED UP.
STEPPED OFF THE LINE.
NOW HE SITS BEHIND A DESK.
STONED.
OVERWEIGHT.
PARANOID.
EVIL.

ALL THE THINGS
THAT HE SOUGHT TO DESTROY,
HE BECAME.
THE GOLDEN PARASITE
SHAKES HIS FIST IN TRIUMPH.
AND RACKS UP ANOTHER ONE.
I THINK OF HIM SOMETIMES.
WONDERING WHEN
HE WILL PULL DOWN
ONE LAST SHOT AT REALITY.
GOODBYE. GOODBYE.
SWEEP YOUR ASHES OUT THE DOOR.
YEAH KILL YOURSELF
BUT NOT HERE.
OK WELL DO IT HERE,
BUT COULD YOU WAIT
FOR A COMMERCIAL BREAK?
THE GOLDEN PARASITE.
GLEAMING IN THE SUN.
HELL YES TURN IT UP.
BUT DON'T GET OUT OF LINE.
COME ON IN.
GET DESTROYED.
THAT WISE-ASS KID.
SIX MONTHS IN THE WOMB.
SOMEHOW THE LITTLE BASTARD
GOT A FAX IN THERE.
WORKED OUT
A THREE MOVIE DEAL.
SUED HIS PARENTS.
COMPLAINED ABOUT THE FOOD.
SAID THAT THE PCP SHE WAS DOING
GAVE HIM THE WORST HEADACHE.
THINGS ARE DIFFERENT NOW.
THE WATER TASTES FUNNY.
EASIER TO GET A BULLET
THAN A GOOD CUP OF COFFEE.

Taken from "THE JACKASS THEORY".

"WAYS TO DIE"

Henry Rollins

#3 WHEN SHE VOMITS I GO WILD

#63 YOUR DICK IS IN YOUR HAND NOT HERS

#87 MY FATHER, BURNT CORPSE, BODY BAG

#101 SHE'S LATE FOR WORK, PREGNANT AND FULL OF HATE

#207 SHE COULD FUCK ME OR KILL ME I WOULDN'T CARE

#230 MY BODY IS MY ENEMY

#349 SHE GOT RAPED FOR A LIVING

#419 HIGHWAY CAT MOUSE PIG MACHINE RETARD

#431 YOUR DAUGHTER TASTES GOOD

#503 YOU WANT PEACE? FILL THE STREETS WITH BLOOD

#522 SPEEDING LIKE A BULLET FALLING LIKE A TEAR

#657 SHE DESTROYS MEN I AM A BOY

#769 SHE SWORE HIS TONGUE WAS FROM HELL

#802 ALL MY WOMEN HAVE HAD ABORTIONS

#851 FIRST NIGHT MARRIED; DOUBLE BED DOUBLE SUICIDE

#933 MEN CLUNG TO HER LIKE DROWNING RATS

#959 SHE SHOT HERSELF FOR MY BIRTHDAY PRESENT

Taken from "THE JACKASS THEORY".

"RED HEDZ"
(*extracts*)

Michael Paul Peter

Paul's body aches.
He can feel pain...that should be a good sign.
Feeling pain should be proof in itself that he isn't dead.
Proof at least that he isn't in Heaven.
Such crudities as pain or pleasure would never be allowed in *that* sickly-shining paradise.
On the other hand, he could have landed in the festering bowels of Hell.
He opens one adventurous eye to check.

Nope, there's his ever-faithful LED digital clock.
Red-eyed sentinel of time standing guard in the darkness.
It's eyes flash 9.00 AM.
"Can't imagine they'd have those down there, anyway... they'd melt."
He laughs to himself.
As he laughs, his Adam's apple knocks against someç^Jtight restriction.

He tries to move his right hand down to feel what it is, but it is caught on something.
He looks up at the hand...it is securely taped to the headboard.
So is his other.
He lifts his head, looking down towards his feet.

He is naked and his feet are restrained with fine, steel wire.
He can see one long, silver wire leading from his neck, down the left side of the bed and into the wall-socket by the door.
Where a gangrene-hand is poised at the switch.
His eyes track up the discoloured arm to the owner's

face.
Jane's face.
Jane's green, putrescent face.
Her black soulless eyes staring through his.
He tries to speak.
Sees her finger move.
Everything turns to instantaneous pain.

*****

Paul's head is buzzing maddeningly.
His ears refuse to work.
His teeth are tight, like arthritic hands.
Little bits of chipped-off enamel under his tongue irritate him.
He opens his eyes, unclenching the lead-encrusted lids with a gargantuan act of will.

"You'll thank me for that, one day..," she mouths, towering over him, tensely waving a fist-held Stanley knife at him.
She looks down at his groin.
His cock is laid back on his stomach, swollen, stiff.
She grabs it and wrenches the skin down, exposing the head.
"Aaah!"
Without warning, she flicks the blade across the tip of the glans.

Hot blood jets out.
She takes it into her mouth and spits the blood onto his chest.
Coughing up large clots.
She lets go of his cock.

It flops back onto his stomach, spewing the scalding blood up onto his chest.
Jane rubs her hands up through the sluicing gore.
It splashes into his eyes, blinding him.
Paul squirms in the intense pain.

He feels her trying to mount him and attempts to knee her.
Struggling to jerk the knee up with enough force.
The restraining wires tighten round his ankles, cutting deep into the Achilles tendons.
His attempt merely nudges her inner thigh, angering her even more.

His mouth stretches wide to scream away pain as the tendons that tense his thighs are sliced through.
His legs go limp.
A hand grabs him by the hair.
He feels the point of steel at his left temple.

Slowly, the blade is dragged across the whole width of his brow, grinding against the bone.
The blood like hot, black coffee seeps down past his ears.
Ribs locked as he tries desperately to push out a scream.
Jane jams the knife down into his open mouth, bisecting the soft-palate uvula, the blade lodging in the back of his throat.

Paul jerks awake.
His body shivering and clammy.
He looks at the clock: 8.46 AM.
Jane is in bed beside him, her arm laid heavily across his throat.
Carefully, he wriggles free of it and shuffles round in bed.
Something feels wet near his leg.

He puts a hand down to feel what it may be.
Touches a wetness and rubs his fingertips together.
Makes a face.
He gets out of bed and pulls back the covers a little.
The tell-tale signs of sleep-ejaculation stare up at him, smug and cynical.
He replaces the covers, careful not to wake Jane, and

leaves the bedroom, closing the door softly behind him.
Into the bathroom, he washes the tacky mess from his leg and splashes water, as quietly as possible, onto his rough face.
"You need a shave."
Running his wet fingers through his hair and brushing it back off his face, he tiptoes through the living-room towards the kitchen.

As he is creeping through the living-room, he sees the discarded shirt on the couch. He picks it up and slips it on, attempting to fasten the buttons.
He looks down.
No buttons.
He goes through into the kitchen and eases the fridge-door open.
"Pernod...I knew you'd still be there."
He takes out the bottle of Pernod, leaving the fridge-door ajar.
The bottle gives out a really satisfying gurgle as he shakes it, indicating more than half a litre of the thick liquor waiting to anaesthetize any confusion.
He kisses the bottle, gets a large tumbler and pours a substantial measure into it.
He bends down into the fridge and finds the black-currant cordial at the back.
Topping up his glass with the dark, purple syrup, he takes a sip of his concoction and smacks his lips at the kick.

Into the living-room, he wanders around and flops down into the centre of the couch.
Brings his left foot up onto the seat.
Tucking it under his right knee.
Leans back, balancing the tumbler on the inside of his left knee, and lets his arms fall across the back of the couch.
Still somewhat shell-shocked, he gazes out through the open blinds.

A hazy sun-lit sky claws numb-fingered at the window.

Paul grips the glass firmly in his hand and knocks back a good half of the sweet nectar.
"God, you're a wreck, Paul," he remarks aloud.
"You know, you're not far wrong," he smirks.
"Have a drink."
"Don't mind if I do." He takes another drink and drains the glass.
"Have another."
"Thank you, I think I will."
He is getting up to refill his glass when a frenzied burst of knuckle-raps bombards the front door.
He tiptoes balletically over to the door and opens it.
Sue is stood in the corridor, finger pointing, mouth poised, ready to shout.
Paul puts his hand over her open mouth to stifle her yells for fear of waking Jane.
Sue bites the suppressing hand.
He pulls it back, shaking it.

In a firm, steady tone, Sue shouts,
"PAUL Kasparek..."
He looks at her and flashes a glance at the bedroom door.
"YOU..."
He scowls at her then back to the bedroom.
"...are an ABSOLUTE..."
Sue is shouting with rising vehemence. Paul's gaze flicks between her and the bedroom door.
"SHI..."
He turns to quieten her and finds himself looking at the empty, dimly-lit corridor.
The sudden coldness of someone walking over his grave courses through the length of his body.

*****

Paul is sat on the couch.

His legs tucked to one side.
The plate in one hand.
Nibbling at the last slice of cheese-on-toast held in the other.
The TV is on...some game show.
The volume is turned down to almost inaudible.
Spot the difference in entertainment value...see!
He picks up the remote from the arm of the couch and flicks through the channels.

Jane pads through to the bathroom, leaving the door slightly ajar.
Then it hits him...
He sniffs the air three times, and the beauty of the aroma almost knocks him out.

He lays the empty plate down on the floor and rises to his feet.
Following the scent into the hissing steam of the bathroom.
The shower curtain is drawn.
The scent now chokingly pungent.
His hand rises, shaky with expectation, and slowly, nervously, pulls back the curtain.

Jane, her hands to her head massaging a creamy lather into her hair, looks inquisitively around one of her raised arms.
She smiles an expectant smile.
Paul lets his gaze track up and down her slender body, standing there in his bath, using his shower, his soap bubbles all down her.
Very erotic.
"Well?" she prompts.

Paul undresses there and then, not taking his eyes off her body.
Her supple back.
Her pert little buttocks.

The foam slithering down the back of her legs.

Totally nude, he steps over the side of the bath, into the hot spray.
Kissing the knobbly bones at the back of her neck, then her bony shoulders.
The water collects in his tousled black hair, snaking down his face in wriggling rivulets.
The scent is now almost blindingly, deafeningly overpowering.
A desire rises within him - a desire to hurt, to maim, to *kill.*
"No," he groans through clenched teeth.

Jane turns around fully, resting her hot arms over his shoulders.
As she draws the shower curtains across, she kisses him warmly.
The spray gathers at their heads and cascades between their embrace.
Lubricating the skin between them so that it becomes somehow more pliable, yet no less fragile.
Paul pulls his head back, shaking it in the spray and growls, "No!"
The water collects in his open mouth and gushes over his chin in a heavy spill.
An intoxicating anger welling up inside him.
A fist punching up from deep in the pit of his stomach "No!" A shout.
Jane looks at him unblinkingly through the constantly shimmering shroud of water,
"Just do it!"

She drops her hands to his back.
Slowly digging the nails in on each side of his spine.
Paul lets out a short "Ah!" and Jane lunges forward.
Her mouth biting at the inside of Paul's open mouth.
Tearing away his lower lip.
Whilst pulling her claws horizontally away from his spine.

Dredging up eight deep trenches.
The nails grating against his ribs as they slowly drag across his back.

Paul can feel a heat that flows from the left side of his mouth down his neck.
His boiling back slinking past his buttocks.
Hot sulphuric acid kissing the channel between the cheeks, on down the inside of his thighs to the bath below.
Paul screams and struggles free of her arms.
Holds them by the wrists.
He raises them up above her head.
Jane stares passionately into his eyes,
"Oh, that was *fun*. Come on, *Loverboy*."

Paul shifts his grip to her elbows and pushes her arms back over her head so that she over-balances, nearly slipping on the suds.
Instead, her hands hit the wall behind her.
Paul keeps pushing.
The hands keep moving...*driven into the wall.*

He pushes harder, until she is elbow-deep in the solid concrete.
Then lets go.
She hangs there from her forearms, kicking her legs and shouting.
"You cheating bastard!"
Her upper arms at either side of her screaming face.

Paul fights her legs with his arms and kisses her translucent body.
The network of veins now clearly visible.
He moves up to kiss her abusive, snarling mouth.
She snaps at him.
He presses his aroused cock up against her, but her legs are tightly crossed.
Angrily, he wriggles his hips, desperate to find a way in.

No way.

His attention moves again to Jane's grimacing face.
She arrogantly brings her face up to his and spits in it.
Paul shakes the dangling gob of spittle from his face then forces his mouth down onto the back of her left arm as she snaps at his ear.
Down the back of the arm he bites, until he reaches the glistening armpit.
His teeth dig into the pliable flesh and pull away a long strip.
Exposing the ribs on that side.
Jane moans in a sick, pleasurable way as the flap of skin dangles over her hip.

Paul dodges round her sneering face to the other armpit and repeats the act, spitting out blood and pushing flesh from between his teeth with his tongue.

Jane writhes in the ecstasy of such degradation.
Her body switching violently from left to right.
The flaps of newly-ripped skin, wildly-thrashing drunken wings, slapping across Paul's back.
Their mixed blood splashing up onto the shower-curtain and wriggling down the back of Paul's legs.
The bath is now ankle-deep in gore.
Paul kisses Jane's chest with the tatters of his mouth leaving a bloody kiss-mark to be sluiced away.
Once again, he presses his cock against her.
He feels a certain submission.
A slight parting of the legs.
He looks longingly into her fierce eyes.
She nods slowly and Paul feels her legs open a little more.
Excitedly, he moves his face closer to hers.
Still gazing into her eyes.
Expectation running at a peak.
Without warning, her forehead crashes down into his pleading face, onto the bridge of his nose.

Paul flies backwards.
Windmilling.
Slipping on the soapy gore and tumbling out through the curtain onto the bathroom floor.

He struggles to his feet, cupping his face in both hands.
Doubled over in pain.
He slowly lowers his hands...
Normality.
Jane is standing above him, still showering, her head a ball of foam.
"Clumsy." She holds out a soapy hand.
Paul takes it, hesitantly.
Straightening up.

He steps over the side of the bath back into the foamy water and allows Jane to massage his aching back. Kissing his forehead and giving his buttocks a playful squeeze.
"We have just unwrapped the second package...slightly larger than the first. Could you feel the dimensions shifting?"
"I...I don't know. It was all too real. My...my body still aches."
"Reality, my dear, is only perception. Perception, merely the sum of certain sensory functions set alongside an illusory timescale. Nothing more, nothing less exists but *your* perception of reality..."

After drying himself off, Paul, looking in the mirror, notices a jagged red line running from the corner of his mouth, losing itself in the shadow underneath his bottom lip.
He touches it, stretching the skin.
Jane is watching, and comforts him,
"Orh, my poor baby."
"Oh, I'll survive. There's nothing too disfiguring there."

He touches it again, pressing his tongue behind the lip, "Looks quite macho."
"Not that," Jane replies. "*These*," delicately touching his back.
He flinches, jerking his back straight.
Straining to look back over his shoulder at the mirror
"What the Hell's that?"

Four fresh scratches.
Either side of his spine.
Scored, horizontally, across his back.
"Stay there, I'll get something for it," she commands, running out of the bathroom.
Paul shouts,
"There's some Germoline in the kitchen. Second drawer, next to the sink...a pink tube!"

Jane returns promptly, inspecting something about the size of a small tube of toothpaste. She shows it to him. "This it?"
"Yeah, hurry up, this is killing me now."
She unscrews the cap and squeezes a long, white worm onto her fingertips. "Ready?"
"Yeah...go on, then!"
Jane dabs her fingers on the tender scars,
"I don't know how this could have happened...you see, the beauty of our secret room is, it *isn't* physical. The room only has one function...to let us witness the fun, not take take part in it. We ought to be completely protected. I just don't get it..."
"Typical."
"What!?"
"Oh, nothing. Look, I'm knackered. Have you finished back there yet?"
Jane slaps his back, "Guess so."
Paul flinches.
"Right, I'm off to bed...don't be long."

"VIXEN-NAKED ULTRA-LUNCHEON"

Michael Paul Peter

It was hot and humid that day in Central London. The balmy air was pressing my damp undergarments to my flesh. This memory of the complementary sensations of disgust and delight that clothed my sweaty predicament, at first a steel-edge reminder of subsequent perfunctory events is now, only twenty-four hours later, a faded and *yes* jaded bastard-son lost to the turmoil of my wonderful and fortuitous reunion late in the afternoon of March 15th 1998.

I had not long since that afternoon, if my flaccid recollections can be relied upon, terminated my employ at the dank and dreary broomcupboard offices of the District Surveyors in Clerkenwell, having exchanged more than a few rather loudly slanderous remarks with my superior upon my final exit, when I happened upon an old cricket-team chum from my studious childhood years as a hardened boarder at Brighton Grammar School.

An enchanted and stoic establishment dedicated to the honourable pursuit of intellectual excellence and comic perversity, that to this haunted day invokes the brain-burning taste of Death Camp soil after the "fog" had settled.

A minor paradise of calculus and cocksucking; in that order.

"Foxhead!" The mystery figure had hailed from across the tumultuous street, thick with groaning, tyke-hauled barrows laden with tubs of donkey-lard, en route to Farringdon Station and all points North.

Initially, I believe, I had picked up my pace somewhat and had pulled my bowler down over my eyes. Perchance my addressor was a debt collector I had up until now managed to evade, or a spurned husband intent on sweet revenge after my name had been innocently cited at the flashpoint of some matrimonial arraignment to which I was hitherto oblivious.

Then, suddenly, realising Foxhead was a name with which I had not been associated since my aforementioned schooldays, I halted abruptly and turned to face my hailor.

He was a tall fellow; gangly-looking as he skipped a loping stride through the perilous wheels and negotiated his navy woolen cape in the aftertow.

Conscientious to keep his footing on the uneven, ill-maintained and dog-shit slick old road.

"Foxhead! It *is* you!" his taut face beamed.

I must have been wearing rather a serious face, for he laughed aloud, tossing back his head in his customarily flamboyant manner; a single gesture so vivid it necessitated no further interrogation.

"Gleeson!" I exclaimed, launching myself arms-wide into his embrace and hugging him to me.

We laughed like thorough-bred lunatics for the better part of a minute; passers-by forcing sheepish grimaces at our mad display.

"But my, how you've grown," I commented.

"Chest high." He broke free, masturbating air.

"Foolish man...I mean, you were always such a..."

"Shrimp? Yes. I admit it. I was a thimble of urine. Cheeks like peaches." He made a fat face.

"Indeed. Where did it all go?"

~The weight? Fucked it off!" he bawled, as a fragile-looking femme glided coyly by.

To my shame, I laughed; aloud. We both laughed, long and loud, intoxicated by each other's spirits.

"And me so lean. So athletic. So hungry-looking," I added between raucous gasps. It was not until I had regained my composure sufficiently that I recognised that all-too-memorable look of effete dread in Gleeson's eyes.

"Easy now..," I remarked, "What could so grieve one so Mercurial of nature as your good self?"

Gleeson suddenly and inexplicably let a big wide grin crawl all the way across his pallid face from ear to ear. A supernatural feat of physiognomy.

"I.. err...seem to have stumbled upon a magnificent

discovery. A purgative for the amoral soul the like of which few mortal men have sampled. Food of the Gods, man. And of their darker halves, no doubt..."

"In plain English."

"Like a fucking eggshell, man," he giggled unrestrainedly. "Feet the size of prawns. The future. Oranges and Cinnamon..."

"Wait, wait..." I tried to calm him.

At length his mania subsided.

"You're not on business of any sort?" he asked, anxiously checking his pocketwatch.

"No. Actually, I was just..."

"Splendid!" He motioned with a sweeping gesture of his white-gloved hands for us to move on, linking arms with me in public. "So much to catch up on. Senile though the days are." He tugged my cheek boyishly. "It's the whorehouse for this couple of war-horses. Merry maids. Copious flagons of ale. The telling of the tale is a snorting foot-fetish." He hooted; lost, I believed, to the insane humour of his own privately-distorted world.

So, after hailing a passing rickshaw and enduring the spine-shattering helterskelter round the seedier parts of this already filthy city, we drew up at the gated entrance to a large estate that sat back away from the main drag the way an old man hunched before the fire leans back on one buttock to blast forth and ignite a methane holocaust, in whose sad blue flames he may see the shimmering faces of lost and former loves - and, perchance, a glimpse of pussy. Not an inviting sight at the best of times, which - considering our sinister locale and the encroaching evening - these were quite obviously not.

Gleeson flipped a column of punched-out florins at the panting 'shaw-punk. "Hey up, Nutcracker, away and fetch some choice bones for your good lady wife. Now then, Foxhead; shall we dine?" With an undersea glance he ushered me enthusiastically down to the sewer which ran along by the cart's metal-rimmed wooden wheels, blind to both the stench and the depth of the effluent he was ankle-deep in. "Come. Hurry."

Taking his gloved hand I stepped reluctantly down from my clean dry elevation and into this slaking ordure. A tingle of fear shot through me as I thought at first that I had lost my feet to the slime. Gleeson as ever had anticipated this and readjusted his hold, clenching my wrist so it threatened to snap, and helped me onto the pavement.

With the rickshaw making a suspiciously hasty get-away and me stamping whatever the Hell it was from my only pair of presentable shoes, Gleeson busied himself with the bell built into the Gothic, marble-column gateposts. "Battleships lost at sea..." he gleamed as I approached him. "Don't look so afraid, wee Foxhead," he continued. "Anyone would think this was your first time on hallowed ground."

I suppose he had already clocked the dread in my eyes. I denied the insinuation outright. "How dare one be so bold!"

"Yes sir." He punched my left shoulder. In the dim distance, a crumpled-over figure carrying a feeble lantern was making his funereal way down the gravel path towards us.

"Doctor White," the lantern-carrier greeted my schoolchum, "How kind of you to greet us with your distinguished presence."

"Doctor!?" I exclaimed, as the wretch wrestled with the cumbersome gate.

"Duke, this my very hairswidth friend, Vincent Lavender - Foxhead as he is to be addressed," Gleeson introduced me.

"I am privileged, Foxhead." He extended a weak and arthritis-ridden claw, which I shook tentatively.

"Now..." Gleeson gathered me under his wing, "...this here is the Duke of New York. That's what they call this place, you know. New Fucking York." He roared with laughter.

Inside the "brothel" I was met by such unrestrained sights of carnality as of some demonic debauch in honour of Satan himself. My clothes, soiled and sticky as ther were, were quickly peeled from me by a trio of naked ladies wearing false pigheads; grunting with swinish, mud-swilling pleasure at my fast-approaching nudity. Gleeson watching the rape bemused as I frantically clutched at my socks and gaiters.

All about me. Men. Women. Children. And, to my astonishment, their *pets*, shaven of all body hair, were indulging in such vile acts of degradation that I feel sick to my stomach even now. Ah, to taste again that virginal vomit...Shhh, who's that? Eerie horror sounds fall away silent.

So, with Gleeson as my lowly guide, I was shown more of this establishment's lurid clientele and voracious, low-life acts.

Passing one open door from which frenzied shouts were emanating I halted to witness a crowd of baying gentry, on their knees before a baited grizzly-bear cub that was being set upon by a pack of seven little naked girls with Chinese finger-hooks and razor-belts; their sobs of pain eaten up by the viewing rabble; their white bodies ripped beyond recognition by the cub's claws; their tiny breasts sliced open, mauled into grotesque mammary grins; their bald heads tattooed with obscure calligraphics. The arousal of the bear-cub aptly illustrated by the angle of its fleshy erection; immune, it seemed, to the multiple lacerations along its throbbing length.

The girls performing balletic leg-lifts, showing off their blood-red pudendae to the audience and urinating bright green when they were inadvertently caught in the horny creature's malicious embrace.

"Piquant," Gleeson glimmered; deriding.

On past many other doors down a panelled corridor, all of them firmly closed on their atrocities, to an open door four from the end on the left. Gleeson elegantly curtsying his buck-naked request for my entry into the room beyond.

I remember standing there in my socks and gaiters, physically shaking, afraid to move, nailed to the shagpile by the apprehension of what revolting horrors lay ahead.

"Foxhead!" Gleeson suddenly shouted, jolting me from my torpor, "Any time before the Solstice!" And he smiled that utterly insane smile that I'm now convinced he had been conscientiously perfecting since his graduation from Brighton Grammar.

Inside the spacious boudoir, soft-lit in violet, was a luxuriant double divan dressed in jaune silk sheets and sporting numerous pillows fashioned from a similar, if not identical, fabric. There was a pungent claustrophobia to the air; a fruity perfume that like an eel or snake wriggled and slithered its nauseating way down into the lungs with my each shallow breath.

"Ha!" jeered Gleeson, "Sentimentalists swallowing their mothers in Summer. Sit, man, sit." He closed the oaken door firmly behind me. "Drink?" he asked.

Again I must have shown a strange face, for he added: "I'll take that as a yes, then shall I?"

I nodded madly. My palms wet with perspiration. As was my top lip; a family trait, the wet upper lip. Always thought that was very Freudian; or maybe Jungian.

The door swung, unannounced and impromptu, ajar.

Startling me so that I let out a shout which made Gleeson drop the decanter he was emptying into two large crystal tumblers. Whilst in through the open door there swept, like Autumn leaves in a stiff breeze, the naked female trio who had so professionally stripped me. Their regimental manner unnerves me still.

They shooed Gleeson away from his cursing and onto the bed, softly laying him down beside where I, in my highly bothered state, had been laid out. I had not protested at their orders nor, at first, had I noticed that as well as the pighead masks they wore, their breasts, large and round and white as I remembered, had been transplanted with baaing heads of ewe.

Amazing trick - I thought at the time.

Time seemed to linger idly by, like a bellboy impatiently awaiting his tip. One of our "hostesses" left the room under no obvious instruction, returning warped moments later with a solid silver tray upon which were arranged a selection of peeled fruits and spices, while the remaining "femmes serviles" had donned lubricant plastic gloves and were busy working Gleeson's and my own dick to a suitable stretch of arousal.

"Fucking amoeboid." Gleeson glimmered; his second favourite face, I declare.

"How's that?" I asked, finding myself less and less able to understand his rapidly thickening dialect.

"Cat smooth. Eggshell slippery," he emoted, grasping the porcine face of his masturbatrix and slobbering luridly into her snuffling snout. Pulling away his bright face, wet with pigspit, and taking with his teeth a fruit segment proferred by the third maiden; my hand-maiden oinking riotously while she wanked. The room had become a menagerous clamour of squeals and laughter and slurps and lechery.

It was at about this point in the farce that, I believe, I first began to panic.

My oinking hand-maiden dipped her masked head over my groin and began sucking my erect dick with her pig-lips. I could feel the tiny pigteeth behind the hairy, rubbery lips, the coarse pork tongue working abrasively against my tender rim. "What the fucking Hell do you think this is!?" I shouted at the very top of my voice, pushing the woman from me and rising, hysterical, to my socked feet.

All four of them were gawping, gobsmacked; utterly astonished at my immature outburst. They were all staring at me, dumbfounded. I noticed one of the girls looking at my erection; standing proud.

"It's a fucking trip, man," announced Gleeson. And all was loud humour once more. "Sewer deep, luncheon hydraulic. Have a piece of orange." He shakily offered me the heavily-laden silver tray.

"Fuck the fruit!" I shouted. This brought even louder laughs, for some sick and twisted reason. "And why have these sluts got pigheads!?" I screamed at the sudden lonely silence. Again four rather serious, accusing countenances.

"You're just being sow-er, man." Faces close to bursting. "Why so pigged off?" Giggles spurting from the sides of mouths. "Oink you happy here?" Immense explosion of mocking laughter.

The orgy resumed. Gleeson, fighting against the amorous tide of swine mouths, hands, sucking breasts of ewe, cunts moist with chuckling, still proferring the silver tray. Eyes brightening ever wider. I felt a cynical hand reaching ashamedly for the fruits; took a lemon-coloured segment and popped it into my mouth.

The room, quite accidentally I believe, fell on its side. I laughed until my lungs ached and I felt my bladder was going to rupture.

It must have taken the girls some time to help me back onto the bouncing jocularity of the divan, for as I was welcomed back into the many female arms a feverish, sweating heat had befallen me, and every other around me.

I remember finding this most amusing.

And as pigheads and eweheads sucked and slurped at my cock; my mouth; my ears; my bollocks; my toes; my fucking toes...and having thought "my fucking toes", in a trice was one of my rampant escorts' boiling cunts engulfing my left foot. She took me in to the ankle, head back, the muscles of her arms veined and pumped up from pulling me in. Though I could no longer see, since there was a ewebreast before my eyes into which I had a mad compulsion to insert my tongue, I could feel my shin slipping further into the woman. I could feel the hairs on my leg brushing inside her uterus, pressing up on her womb.

My toes touching...her *ribs*?!?

I shot to a seated attention. She was there, on her back; legs in the air; my left foot now swallowed up to the fucking knee...ah, not again I thought, having made the metaphorical mistake and having my leg disappear inside her body to the thigh.

Hot hands pulled me back to the bed. I ignored them

and looked to my immediate left.

Gleeson was on his back, face contorted with perverse pleasure as the woman rode him, her bleating breasts and snuffling snout utterly fiendish. Suddenly from the open door came another naked maiden.

But she was very different.

Her Chinese head was bald of hair, and bore only the most basic suggestion of features. Her skin was pale; bleach-white. As sickly a shade as I've ever witnessed. Colour aside, she seemed physically normal until she strolled round to Gleeson's side of the bed. Haunting the place usually set aside for pubics was a small elephant's head complete with nervously flapping veiny ears, curved ivory tusks and, jutting from the pubic bone above her vaginal mouth, a long and inquisitive trunk.

"I can smell your thoughts, you naughty boy," the Chinese woman confessed as her pubic snorkel tasted his forehead exploratively.

"I *know*." Gleeson glimmered and gleamed, shuffling to lay across the bed, his head slung over one edge; "And I want you to screw them. Work me over, you honey." Having given this request he took the trunk in hand and guided it down his own throat. Sucking her off while she smiled at me in her polite Oriental way. Gleeson bucking with choking ecstasy beneath her.

She extricated the trunk with a flick of her slender hips; Gleeson like a hungry fledgeling champing for more. "Come on, give me some more of that. Fuck my eggshell brains out."

The look she gave him would have turned flame to ice. And, though close to orgasm myself, I could not avert my eyes from this battle of wills in order to enjoy my own pleasure. She took his head by the ears. Gleeson's mouth opening and closing impatiently. But instead of plunging the trunk in, she impaled the lethal tusks into the top of his skull. Gleeson let out such a horrendous and horrific scream that I ejaculated with shock, my body fighting peristaltics as I watched on; enthralled.

Ruthlessly, the Chinese woman impaled the tusks once more into his broken head, screwing his brains to pulp. On went the destruction, Gleeson's face splitting, nose dividing, until at the height of the brain-curdling his body jolted; as a result of the elephant head in his cranium, or the strange woman jumping up and down on his cock, I know not.

But jolt he did; throwing off his sex-rider; hurling aside the Chinese; a gushing deluge of excreta ejaculating from his gaping brainpan.

"Fucking Egg Shell!!" he screamed, as out of the cranial fissure three foetal forms, covered in silky grey fur, flopped. Siamese triplets joined at the point of the lacerations they were busy inflicting on each other with claws and teeth and desire. All red and dripping bodies matting black in the feeding frenzy.

The trio crashed to a slushing mess by the unseated pighead woman as she struggled to regain her bearings through the fog between her ears. Her pink head sporting a neat bruise, cut to a gaping lump. Instinctively, like a shark in the presence of blood, the trio - one frenzied form - pounced upon the dazed woman. Gouging and gnashing out great wet burning bleeding chunks of flesh. Her porkhead squealing. Ewebreasts protesting with deafening bleats. Her plastic-gloved hands punching gaping wounds through fur.

Pulling back bloody stumps.

To my further astonishment, the remaining women seemed totally oblivious to the death of one of their own. The woman with my entire left leg up her hot cunt was still bucking like fury. I cared not that my socked foot was peeping out of her mouth. Cared not that her fingers were pulling off the sock and gaiter so that her thin pink tongue could protrude between the toes; cared not for the Chinese bitch who had turned over the dead carcass of Gleeson White and perched herself behind his bare arse, and had shoved her elephant trunk deep inside his anus only to pull it out, lick brown faeces from the wrinkled leathery tip with her cunt-mouth then shove it into that effluent passage once more. Cared not for the woman at my prick, wanking me off in all the right ways with her smooth conic fingertips and snuffling in my belly-button for truffles. Cared nothing for the sour stench of sex and slaughter. What disturbed me was the fact that the foetal mass that erupted from Gleeson's brain had reared itself up onto its highest hind legs and was looming drunkenly over that side of the bed, licking its many lips and leering with its many eyes, bringing with it the truly nauseating stench of its punctured-internal-organs-and-shit-soup exhalations.

Ever so casually, it began to topple towards us.

I remember in my daydream scrambling away from the falling hulk. And, as I clambered dizzily to my feet at the door end of the room, witnessing the uncloaking of the truly nightmarish, tearing all my senses to shreds.

The humungus struck the occupants of the bed with a wet and bonecrunching thud. Instantaneously, it tore into the Chinese whore, still buggering the lifeless casing of Gleeson White, with gargantuan glee; ripping her featureless head right from her shoulders. Her spasming trunk, as she fell back off the bed, spurting a gangrenous sewerage high into the room. The far side of the abomination munched great lumps out of the dead Gleeson White, while some other insane part of it devoured a pigheaded whore from the feet up. The look on her porcine features as flint-edged teeth chomped and crunched one of her legs while she kicked out one of its roving eyes with the other; that horrible squeal of her breasts; eyes like bolts of lightning as it sought out and chewed to a pulp her clitoris. The only surviving whore was trapped on the far side of the room, urine trickling down the inside of her white legs.

"Run!!" I shouted, holding out a hand. She looked at me and squealed. That distress call shot through me; chilling. "Quick!!" I urged as the monster on the bed was in momentary respite, busy licking its lips.

"Jump!" No sooner had I screamed that final word than she was leaping over the edge of the bed, grabbing sweatily at my outstretched hand.

Saved.

Until that rash impression turned into yet another disgusting red herring; for as I pulled her to me her pigface began to split, her mouth widening grotesquely, and she was snatched from me, dragged to the beast by a surreally-mutated arm. She squealed and squealed until the top of her head was gnawed off, her manic eyes weeping blood. I turned from the horror and ran into the corridor, which was now carpeted in shrimp fur and husks of salt-cured oyster tendon; bedraggled with barking ropes of giraffe blubber. Each door I frantically yelled at was locked. Even the far door where I had espied the baiting of girls and bear was locked; from the inside.

I raced into the reception area but it was devoid of men, women, children or even their shaven pets. The air stank of violets. I threw up onto a highly-polished circular ebony dining table I had failed to notice on my disrobed arrival.

The carriage clock in the corner by the front door proclaimed a deafening midnight.

As the chimes rang out their solemn knell I shook the locked door in its frame until the glass shattered, showering my naked body and bare left foot with shards of glass. I fell back to the wooden floor, spitting curses. My trembling hands picking out bits of jagged glass from my knees, shins and feet. The pain unbelievable.

There was a rasping sound behind me. I spun round.

There, lumbering its horrendous way towards me on all fours, was Gleeson White. His bare back was scarred and potted from his attempts to escape. His arms dislocated, it seemed, from his shouldwrs black with bruises. When he raised his buckled and twisted head I thought I would die on the spot.

The skull was distorted to elephantine proportions. Big grey ears a-flapping, cooling the searing heat of his wounds. Its ivory tusks curved up out of his eye-sockets, the eyeballs still a-watching, perched at the ends.

He opened his mouth and a loud trumpet sounded as a long grey trunk unravelled, impersonating his tongue, and spat a meaty splatter of blood at me. His arms dislocated further from his shoulders, grinding gristle, and just hung by his sides as he mechanically rose to his feet. His dick and bollocks had been bitten off, and in their place, grafted into his skin, was a slobbering pighead; bleating like an electrocuted lambkin.

I scrambled back through the shattered glass, tearing up my hands and lacerating my buttocks. Impaling my bleeding palms on the splintered glass door-frame, I dragged my pain-racked body through to the heavy front door, and fought with the lock.

Hooves charged me from behind. I turned, terrified at what my ears purported. And my eyes at last saw Gleeson White for the Satanic demon that he was. His skin now all but flayed off; bleeding lakes. His eye-tusks directed at my chest as I...

Well, actually, I have lied.

I have lived my last dying hours a lie, to discourage the sad recurrence of their memory.

The truth, my good friend, is an abysmal catalogue of insult piled high upon injury. The horrors I experienced as the roiling mass of mutated flesh and bone and terror fell towards me, as I struggled to extricate my leg from that whore's greedy cunt, is too great a burden.

You cannot imagine the pain, the artificially-prolonged humiliation I underwent in that fucking room. Nothing quite as heroic as a death struggle, I'm afraid.

My constitution, you see, has never been that strong, and the effect of my panic regurgitated the vile symptoms of a recurring illness with which I am cursed. To tell the truth, the fucking thing fell right on top of me, breaking my rib-cage and snapping my spine. It devoured all the women but, for some insufferable reason, left me unscathed as I writhed in my agony. It also left Gleeson White's dead body where it lay, and I had to suffer his rapid, nauseous decay for many hours.

My lungs are now haemorrhaging regularly. Christ, I feel I may choke on these damn bloodclots at any minute. From below, the chiming of midnight sounds.

Oh, the agony. How long must I stay here, incapacitated as I am, gulping my fate? Again, those ever-present, eerie sounds make me shudder.

"Why am I here!?" I splutter.

Someone appears at the door.

"*Foxhead*!" The bent-over old man addresses me. I strain to make out who it is. Recognition.

"Duke. Help me."

"Can't do that, sir. More than my job's worth." He smiles apologetically as I again cough up a meaty haemorrhage.

"Please. Help me," I beg.

He purses his parched lips. "Oh, I don't know sir."

"Please. For pity's sake."

"Battleships lost at sea..." he mutters.

"What was that?" I cough restrainedly.

"Sorry, sir?"

"That. That thing. Battleships. What is that? I've heard that before."

"It's an old sailor's saying, sir." He raises his snowy eyebrows. I urge him on with my eyes; pleading.

"Well..." he begins, "Battleships lost at sea, sir, rarely surface." He shrugs. And dutifully pulls the door closed.

Locking it on my screaming, coughing, shouting, choking death.

Taken from "RED STAINS".

"PASSION"

John Smith

Bannen glanced at the water pitcher on the bedside cabinet and licked his lips. They felt as if someone had left matches to burn out on them. He sighed and went back to looking at the ceiling.

The nurse had told him Laing would be in later to explain what he was still doing alive, but that was over an hour ago and he'd heard nothing since. He moved his attention to the stain in the corner of the room, tracing its outline in his head to try and distract himself from the ache of his arms. It was the third time he'd tried to kill himself this way; he knew what to expect when the drugs wore off. The cramps were the worst, insects shuttling up and down under his skin, trying to unpick the stitches.

"Fuck," he said. His voice was dry, cracked, but he enjoyed its familiarity. He chanted the word slowly, speeding up, trying to conjure anger from the red place inside him but finding it empty.

If I could just move my arms, he thought. It's these fucking bandages. They're like fucking plaster casts.

He closed his eyes and replayed his suicide: watched the razor blade rule a line from wrist to elbow. He wondered whether he should try paracetamol next time, but knew he never would. An overdose was too clean, too impersonal. It was the sight of blood on skin that made him real. It always had.

He was on the verge of sleep when the sister arrived. He remembered her from the last time: fat and pale, skin like freshly-broken bread. She reminded him, obscenely, of his father.

"How are you feeling, Michael?"

She stood over him, smoothing out his pillows. He wondered if her hands would come away slick with blood, but of course they didn't. Why should they?

"Will you get me a drink?"

"In a second."
"Just some water."
She smiled and filled a glass but left it on the cabinet out of reach.
"Nurse Lowndes said you were back again." Her lips were the colour of liver. Spittle danced across them and was licked away. "Don't you remember what you told us the last time you were here?"
"I'm not simple. You don't have to talk to me like I'm simple, you know?"
Her smile wavered, tightened. "We're not just here for your benefit, Michael. Most people are in here because they need to be."
"Go and fuck yourself."
"I'm sure Dr.Cashman will want a word with you when he gets in tomorrow."
"He can go and fuck himself, too."
The sister moved the glass and pitcher further back on the cabinet. "That's all right, Michael. You get it out of your system. Perhaps you'll be feeling a little more grown up by tomorrow."
He turned away to face the wall. "Twat," he said.

He watched the snow through the window, blowing across the whitened lawns, turning the streetlights into big orange fists. It was on a night like this he'd made his first kill. A girl, wavy auburn hair, who looked twelve or thirteen but was almost certainly younger. Closing his eyes he could see her now: legs flailing, blood splashing the snow. The memory of her smell and the feel of her skin on his lips. His cock was hard in seconds.
If only he had one of the magazines with him. Or better still some middle-class slut perched on the edge of his bed right now. A schoolgirl in a training-bra. He imagined her fighting against him; saw himself strike her in the mouth with both fists; kiss the blood from her mouth.
The room was stifling. Sweat prickled under his arms, in the crooks of his thighs. He kicked back the

sheets but the air was just as hot as that he shared the bed with. The heat crawled over him, pressing close. It was like lying in water. He could feel the blood as it heaved itself through his head, sluggish, as if carrying silt. It slowed his thoughts to a crawl. He wiped the sweat from his forehead then moved his hand down to loosen the front of his pyjamas. His cock jumped up as if on string.

He was masturbating when the door opened. He snatched his hand away as if scalded. An old woman was shuffling into the room, looking dazed, lost. She wore a pink see-through nightdress and her feet were bare. Bannen scrabbled at his pyjamas but his forearms felt weighted, swollen as Popeye's. They barely moved. His cock twitched in the slit of his fly.

"I think you're in the wrong room," he stammered.

The old woman limped towards the side of the bed, unhearing. Her hair was fine and white as cotton. A vein trembled at her temple.

"Do you know where you're supposed to be?" he said, then her hands closed round his cock and squeezed.

Stop her, he told himself. Tell her to stop. But the part within him that was forever hungry kept him silent. All sensation drained out of him and into his cock. The woman closed her lips around it and forced it into her mouth, pushing her head down until he felt the heat at the back of her throat. She stole her hands up across his chest and took hold of his nipples. Her mouth worked on his cock, tighter and faster. He moaned as he felt the hot liquid pressure shiver out from his groin, and his whole body tensed as he came in her mouth. Her gums closed on his cock and she sucked greedily at his come.

Then she pressed her lips against his and slid her tongue between them, passing on the salt-sweetness of his semen. He moved his tongue against hers, drinking in the taste, and her age didn't matter at all. She was a woman, doing what a woman should.

She pulled back and he let her go reluctantly. But she wasn't finished. He watched as she drooled semen into her hand and worked it up into her cunt. Bannen strained for a glimpse of wetness inside but could see nothing for the frantic scrabbling of her fingers. She was like a starved child cramming in food. The fierceness of her movements must have been painful. Sure enough there was a damp tearing sound and blood fell from between her legs. It splashed over her feet; wound down the inside of her thighs like ribbon. When she stepped away she had left two dark footprints on the carpet.

As she reached the door she stopped, her back to him.

"Your mother's here," she said, and left.

Bannen lay idle in the heat, semen drying on his cock, wondering what she'd meant. Of course his mother had died when he was eight, hollowed out by disease, but none of that mattered. He knew by the way the air shimmered and the heat danced in his head that whatever happened while he was here had no connection with reality. A memory slipped into place: his mother smiling, hair the colour of lint, standing on a chair taking apples off a tree. Something swelled in his throat but he swallowed it away as if afraid it would choke him.

A flicker of light in the corner of his eye drew him away from the wall. It was the transfusion bag hanging from its stand beside the bed. Hollows in the plastic caught the fluorescents and threw them back. For a second he thought he saw something move in the bag - a face and two hands pressed against the side - but when he blinked it was only light.

Outside, in the corridor, someone shuffled past.

Unease washed over Bannen. "Hello?" he called, but there was no reply.

Painfully, he propped himself up in bed and pulled the IV needle out of his arm, flinching as it snagged on the bandages. It left a tiny spot of red, like an insect bite. Now the needle was out and he was sitting upright he felt stronger, more sure of himself. He flexed his fingers, a pianist's warm-up exercise. Pins and needles rattled through his tendons but the drugs diluted it, watered it down to a dull ache.

Though his legs were unsteady he managed to stand up. He leaned back against the wall, letting it take his weight. His feet had lost all sensation and he had to stamp them on the floor before any feeling came back. When it did they felt huge, rubbery, as if he was wearing flippers.

He looked at the bloodstain that Rorscached out across the carpet. In the heat and sudden dizziness that washed over him it seemed to move, twisting like a shadow. He saw bodies in that shape, naked, heads thrown back, legs forced wide. Nausea fluttered against him but he turned it away. It was not a sensation he was used to. When he took the girls - pulling their skirts over their heads, working butchery upon their bodies - all he felt was joy. A wild capering joy that had no part in his life at any other time. He was too familiar with violence to be squeamish.

Somewhere outside, amplified by the tiled hospital acoustics, he heard his mother's voice. She was saying his name. It stirred something inside him and it was something like need. Walking unsteadily, arms held out to support himself, he crossed over to the door and went outside.

The corridor was empty except for a surgical trolley near the doors leading out of the ward. The fluorescent lights stuttered above him, set just far enough apart to leave a wedge of shadow between each one. On either side doors lead off to offices or nurses' quarters. They were all closed except for the recreation room. He looked in as he moved past. A TV set seethed with static under a snow-lit window.

He carried on walking, out through the far doors and into the main foyer. Night-lights burned behind hooded iron grilles, bleaching the shadows to sepia. Some of the lights were broken, jagged mouths of bulb bared in sockets. Beneath the smell of disinfectant there was something damp, organic. It was the smell of abandonment. If he hadn't known he might have thought the place had been closed down. Scheduled for demolition, perhaps.

He reached an intersection and stopped. Halfway down one of the corridors there was a dog. It stood watching him, head down, mouth open. Its coat was black except for a patch of white between its front legs. He could hear it panting.

Bannen glanced round, searching for a sign of its owner, but there was no-one. He looked back at the dog. As soon as he was facing it the dog turned round and padded off down the corridor, away from him. Its nails *snik-sniked* across the bare floor. Bannen scanned the corridor one last time then walked on after the dog. Follow the leader, he thought, remembering all the Lassie films he'd seen as a child.

It lead him down corridor after corridor, always the same distance in front of him. Sometimes he'd turn a corner and find that he'd lost it, stop, go back the way he came, searching frantically, filled with unreasoning panic. But the dog would always be waiting for him somewhere. Signs hanging from the ceiling pointed out different areas - PHYSIOTHERAPY, X-RAY, OPERATING THEATRE, RECEPTION - but they continued on the same twisting route, heading deeper into the hospital.

He followed it down a flight of stairs and along a narrow passage lined with lockers. Transparent plastic bags slouched in doorways, filled with empty specimen bottles. Three chairs had their backs against the wall; a magazine lying open on one of the seats showed a battleground littered with bodies. Most of them were children.

Bannen shivered. He pulled his pyjamas closer and hugged himself tightly. The cold floor had slapped all feeling from his feet. Numbness lodged in his arches like pebbles.

In the darkness ahead a girl giggled.

Bannen stopped. The skin at the back of his neck crawled taut; his balls hitched up into his groin as if on wires. He wiped a hand across his lips, tasting semen. He stared past the dog and into the shadows, straining so hard the corner of his eye began to jump, but he could see nothing. Just the frame of a door. Then something was flung at him out of the darkness. It landed at his feet with a soft wet smack. Bannen stared at it for seconds before kneeling to pick it up. It was a white mouse, like the ones they used in laboratories; like the one he'd kept as a child. A red silk ribbon was tied around all four legs, trussing them togeether. Fingers slippery with sweat he started to unpick the knot, looking up every now and again to check the darkness across from him. The mouse had been hollowed out, its insides gone, turning it into a small crimson pouch. There was a gold ring lodged inside.

"It's your mother's."

The voice wavered out of the darkness, slurred, bronchial. "Put it on."

Bannen let the gutted mouse drop to the floor and examined the ring. He wiped the blood off it with a thumb. He didn't need to see the pattern etched into it to know it was his mother's wedding ring.

He looked back into the shadows past the doorframe, and thought he could make out a shape. He took a step forward. Another. Another.

When he found his voice it didn't sound like his at all. "She was wearing this when she was buried. I remember her wearing it."

The darkness giggled again, louder. It had more voices now.

"How did you get it?" he asked.

A light blazed on in front of him, bright as a floodlight. Bannen closed his eyes and covered them with his hands, walling himself in from the glare. He waited until the after-image had faded before opening them again. Warily, he peered out through the slits of his fingers.

After the dimness of the corridors the light was blinding, eating into the sides of the figures like leprosy. They were children, ten or twelve of them, though two were a good head taller than the others. The light shaved them down to skeletons. Framed in front of them, shielded from the bulk of the glare, the dog was silhouetted perfectly, a ragged black stencil. One of the smallest children bent to stroke it.

Bannen put a hand back over his eyes, trying to separate their faces from the light.

"What's going on? What the fuck are you *doing*?"

"We're playing." It was a boy's voice, soprano-soft. The others sniggered as if he'd said something dirty.

As his eyes adjusted to the light Bannen saw that most of them were female: the hips, the fluted waist, the shallow swell of breasts. His cock stirred in his trousers, but he was barely aware of it. He was trying to concentrate on the children. They all seemed familiar, somehow. He squinted at one of them, his gaze moving to the V of her crotch. It was only when he caught sight of the signature he'd left there that he realised why she was so familiar.

He felt a scream well up inside him, a black tarry bubble that threatened to burst his lungs. It was as if he'd breathed in too much air and couldn't breathe it out.

There was movement at the back of the crowd and another figure, taller than the children, stepped out of the light.

Bannen wanted to turn and run before he saw its face, terrified that he'd recognise it. But behind him there was a sticky dragging sound as something slid towards his heels and he stopped suddenly, realising he was trapped. Muscles jumped and bunched in his back. He gathered his shoulders together, expecting something soft to land between them at any second, and stared into the light as if willing it to blind him. The skin twitched at the corner of his eye as if caught on a fish-hook.

From behind the children the figure stepped forward into view. It was the old woman who'd visited him in his room. Impossibly, she was pregnant. Her stomach was huge, scored with veins the thickness of fingers. The skin was so taut it was shiny. As he watched, it rippled with movement as the burden inside shifted its weight.

The old woman laid a hand palm down on her stomach, as flat as arthritis would allow, and looked up at Bannen. "Your mother's here," she said. She sounded almost sorry for him.

Bannen took an involuntary step back and one foot brushed the thing behind him. It was cold, and smooth as wet suede. His skin crawled with disgust but he couldn't have stopped from turning round even if he'd tried. He saw something shapeless and rubbery, the colour of lard. Its back broke into life as it moved, twisting up into spirals of scar tissue. A thigh-wide strip of gristle shrugged up an udder of fatty yellow cones. Bannen tried to move when one slopped towards him but his muscles had locked, welding him in place. A rope of fat closed around one ankle like a tongue.

Over the clamouring panic in his head he heard the old woman speaking. But the words were blurred, a litany of pleas and orders, and it seemed like minutes before he could sort them into anything that made sense.

"Oh, my children, pleasure me now..."

Bannen watched as the crowd closed in on her. She held her arms out from her sides, the light behind her transforming her into some burning martyr. The children circled her slowly, their bodies strobing the light, then drew in. He saw hands rise and fall; heard liquid splash the floor. A few of them worked diligently between her legs, digging upwards. Others tore at her stomach. There was blood and the sound of muscle being peeled off bone. Moaning, her head tipped back, the old woman gathered the children to her. Hands rose and fell, scooping away flesh like mud.

One of the smallest children, a boy, slipped in the blood and was lost in the carousel of bodies. When he saw him next, the boy was forcing his head into the old woman's cunt, trying to clamber back into the womb. Whatever was already in there drew him deeper.

It was as if a signal had been given. The others moved back slowly, reverently, their job finished now that one of them had succeeded. The boy and the woman remained joined like that for seconds, coupled together, mother and child, lovers. Then the boy's body bucked violently. Another convulsion and he had torn free of her cunt. He dropped to his knees, limbs trembling, piss pooling out around him.

There was something in place of his head. It was like a pumpkin, ridged and shiny, grotesquely out of proportion with his body. The old woman slipped forwards, empty as old clothes, and the children lowered her to the floor.

Bannen felt his bowels turn over; the taste of bile scale his throat. He wanted to cough but was afraid that would draw the children's attention. He was terrified they would practice their handiwork on him. There would be justice in that, he thought, and for a moment he considered falling to his knees and begging for his life.

Why shouldn't Isaac turn his hand against Abraham?

There was a murmur from the children and Bannen looked up in time to see the next innovation.

What had been the boy's head had convulsed inwards, splitting from top to bottom. It opened into six segments, a slow languid movement like the opening of a flower. They twitched upwards, flexed, then umbrella'd closed around the boy's waist. Bannen watched as the fist of meat clenched and unclenched, moving further down his body each time, until only his feet were visible. There was a moment of indecency as a skirt of flesh hiked up at one side to show the pulpy red core beneath. The dog moved in and licked it, tail wagging.

In Bannen's head there were a dozen voices, screaming at him to run, to turn round and run and not stop until he was outside, running in the snow. But the silt that filled his limbs had set, turning him to masonry. Only his cock was alive: it pulsed with heat, so hard it was painful.

What terrified him most was that a part of him *wanted* to see this; was entranced by the dripping miracles at work. He had come near to atrocity before, but always using rope and knife and cock. Never in such a fabulous way. He felt as if the very act of seeing this might transform him, turn him into something more than what he already was. Even now he could feel the stitches in his arms moving, as if trying to weave his skin into some strange new garment.

He turned back to the thing in front of the light, rapt. It had grown now, absorbing the children as easily as clay, shaping a torso, limbs, an anvil of a head that jutted from the ruined head. The dog was licking it again, cleaning away clots of blood and skin as if it were a new-born pup.

There were only two children left now, both girls. He recognised them instantly: the long blonde hair as much as the notches he'd carved in their thighs. One had fallen to her knees in worship, and though she'd shat herself in fear she gazed up at the abomination with a beatific smile. It lifted her gently in its spade-like hands and bent her body backwards, touching head to buttocks. Her waist split like paper; her lungs burst with a flat clap. A rib ragged with nerves flipped through the air, drizzling blood. The creature drew back its head and crammed the body clumsily inside. It had to break both legs before it would fit.

The other girl received less attention. The creature simply planted the spurs along its wrists into her shoulder-blade and plucked off her arm. The skin slopped from her back like wallpaper. Spine bared, ribs grating as she exhaled one final time, she pitched onto her face, dead of shock.

As if it were a favourite dish, the dog came last. The creature tipped its upper body back like some graceless limbo-dancer, mouth widening until it took up its entire chest. The dog started to bark as it was lifted by its head, hind legs kicking in mid-air. Then it was dropped into the unzipped mouth. The dog went on barking for seconds after it had been swallowed. Slowly, deliberately, the creature pawed the ground, nails raking up linoleum, and turned to Bannen.

Standing floodlit in the corridor he was immediately aware how exposed he was. He felt as if he was on display, some prime side of beef up for raffle. His erection wilted, so much useless meat. His sphincter loosened as the shit in his bowels turned liquid. Diarrhoea seeped out and traced the line of his arse, warm as a finger.

His legs started to buckle as the creature stumped towards him, but it caught hold of him before he could fall. The surface of its hand was rough as brick and covered with tiny barbs. They tore through his skin like hooks.

Bannen stared up at the creature's face. It was a maze of folds, thick red ridges that looked as if they had been plaited out of coral. He tried to find its eyes in all those twists of flesh. Only when one moved did he realise that was what they were.

"Don't. Please. Please, *don't...*"

He was begging, like the children had begged, like the girls had begged as he cut them, fucked them, even through their screams. He knew now what it was they were afraid of, what it was they saw in him, and he started to cry, ugly wracking sobs that tore into him like meathooks. It was the sound of confession.

"Oh Jesus...Don't kill me. Please. I don't want to die. Those things, all those things I did, I never...I didn't *mean* them..."

It hauled him up until its face was inches from his, and he smelled its breath, cold and sweet. When he looked up he saw blonde hairs stuck in the gore of its lips. He moaned, watched saliva unspool from the corner of its mouth, pink with blood.

"I love you," it said. It cradled his head in its other hand, as if he was a baby being christened, and pulled him nearer. Bannen struggled as the mouth unlatched itself.

He caught a glimpse of teeth - spiked beads rolling in an abacus of gum - then it pressed its face against his and kissed him. He tasted blood; more as his lip tore open on its strings of teeth. He started to struggle then, punching, kicking out with his bare feet, but the creature's mouth remained fixed around his, working crudely away.

As he sucked in air to scream the creature exhaled, breathing out in one cold steady blast. The air kept on coming, filling his lungs, his head. He was dimly aware of blood vessels bursting at the corner of his vision. His cheeks felt wet as his eyes began to bleed.

Just as suddenly he was free. The creature dropped him to the floor and took a step back as if looking at him for the first time. He shuffled away, wiping his eyes with the sleeves of his pyjamas, mopping away blood. He was terrified he'd go blind. That one primal fear over-rode everything else. He didn't see the creature until it was on him, and by then it was too late. A shovel-sized hand was groping between his legs.

This time Bannen screamed. He watched, mesmerised, as the vice of its fingers closed round his cock and balls, and there was a gristly *-snap-* as it took them off.

The agony was huge. Impossible. It filled everything; *was* everything. It slammed through every inch of his body, eating him up and spitting him out in pieces. He put his fist in his mouth to stifle the screaming and bit through the side of his hand without even realising. The pain was too big to let anything else in. It took him somewhere big and white and empty and he drifted there for what seemed like hours.

When it passed - or became bearable - he found he was no longer afraid. His fear had been destroyed, burned out in that brilliant arc-light discharge, leaving him exhausted but strangely cleansed. Almost reborn.

Bannen dragged himself across the floor, hands

clutched over the wound between his legs. He saw the iron grating of an elevator on the other side of the corridor and started to crawl towards it. The horror behind him was forgotten until he felt its breath on the back of his neck. It was like a noose. Its shadow spilled over him, swallowing him up.

He rolled onto his back and stared up at the creature. "*What do you want?*" he screamed. "*Why are you doing this?*" He was crying openly, all pretence at manhood gone. All he felt now was frustration; the rage of a child whose friends refused to play by his rules. "*Why are you doing this?*"

The creature touched his face lightly, brushing away a tear.

"Because I love you," it said.

It was *his* answer. It was his reply to the spittle and shit and tears he'd met each time. They would look up at him, searching for reason in his face, seeing the simplest reason in the world.

"I do this to possess you. I do this to make you mine." The creature put words to his thoughts.

Bannen backed away until he was up against the cage of the elevator, then reached out, scrabbling for the call button. But he was too slow, and one black fist sent him sprawling.

He looked up and saw fresh changes being wrought on the creature's body. Its stomach opened from crotch to diaphragm, exposing a sheet of muscle which peeled itself back like lips. When he saw the guts re-arranging themselves in the darkness he realised with sick horror that it was shaping its own cunt. Fluids ran out of the opening, mouthwash pink, and trickled down the ribs of its thighs. There was the sound of badly-thrown clay as something shrugged itself up from the wetness inside.

Bannen tried to move away but a foot came down on his thigh, pinning him to the floor.

"*See*," the creature said.

He saw. Watched the cock slide out from the mouth of cunt like a piston, swelling as it came. It was the size of a weightlifter's forearm, gunmetal grey, shiny with fluid. Veins ran along its length like blue icing. At its base he saw the complex rigging of tendons and muscles it took to support it.

A child, he called his mother's name.

The foreskin was pulled back suddenly, opening like an eye, and the head glistened in the light, steaming. It was wedge-shaped, the colour of sour cream. A bead of semen had gathered at its tip. The creature wiped it onto the side of its hand and brought it towards Bannen's lips; jerked him back by his hair to make him lick it.

That was when Bannen's nerve broke. He heard it, like a pencil snapping in two, and he was buried alive in panic.

He lashed out with feet and fists, fighting with the clumsiness of a child. His fingers caught the lips of its cunt and he dug in his nails and pulled, tearing out a handful of meat. The creature stepped back, more surprised than hurt, and Bannen scrambled to his feet. His blood-soaked pyjamas had stuck to his thighs; they made a wet sound as they pulled away from his skin.

He felt the creature's face brush his back and kicked out frantically behind him. There was a fire alarm on the wall nearby and he lunged towards it, slammed at the safety glass until it broke. He might have escaped then, might have used precious seconds to get away, but he slipped in the blood that had collected on the floor and lost his balance. The creature caught hold of his wrist as the alarm started ringing, and dragged him round to face it.

"Go *on!*" he screamed. "*Do* it! Fucking *do* it, you bastard! You fucking *cunt!*"

It did it. Teeth ground down to the bone as his hand was snipped off at the wrist. Bannen was too weak to scream. He watched numbly as the bellows bulged beneath its neck, then shrank as the creature exhaled. Felt his arm blow up like a novelty balloon. Heard the tiny understated *-pop-* as his elbow dislocated. Then the skin burst. The bandages blushed a sudden red as the stitches undid themselves. Muscle and skin came unzipped and flopped off the bone like an empty sleeve. Bannen saw what was left and threw up.

There was no need for that, something in his head was saying. That was just gratuitous. There was no need for it. the words found their way to his lips and he mouthed them, over and over, as if they were a chant that would ward off evil. It didn't matter what happened now. He was finished. He could feel himself draining away. The fire alarm was growing fainter, and he followed the sound, let it carry him into the shadows that were rushing in to fill his head.

The creature spat in his face. It was only phlegm but it was enough to raise a flicker of consciousness. He realised, dully, that it wanted him to stay awake for the finishing touches. It was a scene from a dream. A vast engine of sex that was turning his sex against him.

Everything tipped on its side as the creature rolled him onto his back. He saw it, dimly, crouching over him, arms held out like a surgeon. Then it straddled him; tore away his pyjamas; used the spurs on its wrist to enlarge the wound between his legs. He felt the piston of cock slide in, greased with his own blood.

As it fucked him into unconsciousness, Bannen speculated idly on the relationship between sex and death. But realised, as he gazed at the thing standing over him, that he already knew what it was.

"Passion," he said, wondering if it was true that only women died on their backs.

Taken from "RED STAINS".

The CREATION PRESS Catalogue 1991

(All books are softback unless stated otherwise)

"RAISM" James Havoc ISBN 1 871592 00 3
The controversial hymn to satanist Gilles de Rais.
Illustrated by Jim Navajo.
"(Havoc)...is one of the three best poets writing in the English language." - NME.
"A madman to watch." - BLITZ.

"POEMS 1827-49" Edgar Allan Poe ISBN 1 871592 01 1
A collection of his best poetry, illustrated with lithographs by Odilon Redon.

"THE BLACK BOOK" Tony Reed (ed.) ISBN 1 871592 03 8
Extreme dark fantasy stories by new writers. Illus.
"...reminiscent of Roald Dahl after the blast of My Bloody Valentine and some vicious acid" - CUT.

"BODY BAG" Henry Rollins ISBN 1 871592 04 6
A brutal colection of works from the American hard-core hero turned literary terrorist.

"THE JACKASS THEORY" Henry Rollins ISBN 1 871592 05 4
A collection of his most recent work in one volume.

"RED HEDZ" Michael Paul Peter ISBN 1 871592 02 X
Extreme tale of psycho-sexual tyranny and mutation.
"...takes writers like William Burroughs and Clive Barker as merely the starting-point for a mixture of poetry, cut-up fiction, hallucinatory rantings and keenly observed characterisation." - SKELETON CREW.

"CATHEDRAL LUNG" Aaron Williamson ISBN 1 871592 06 2
A volume of ecstatic poetry from the eccentric poet and performer, who is also profoundly deaf.
"Aaron seems to confront his anger by grabbing language by the throat...creates something radically different from most writers." - SOUNDBARRIER.

Forthcoming:

"RED STAINS" Julian Hell (ed.) ISBN 1 871592 08 9
New stories of extreme fantasy and the psycho-sexual imagination. A progression from the "Black Book". Authors include James Havoc, Tony Reed, Michael Paul Peter and John Smith.

"SATANSKIN" James Havoc ISBN 1 871592 10 0
Twenty stories of weird imagination from the young "madman", disclosing an occult world of surrealism, perversity and the bizarre. A limited edition hardback, with cover art by Mike Philbin.

ANNIHILATION PRESS (non-fiction):

"THE VELVET UNDERGROUND" ISBN 1 871592 50 X
Notorious 60's sleaze document that inspired the naming of the legendary New York rock and roll band, whose songs often mirrored its themes of social and sexual sickness.

Forthcoming:

"ED GEIN - PSYCHO" ISBN 1 871592 51 8
Weird, nightmarish but *true* story of murder, grave-robbing, mutilation, necrophilia, cannibalism, and more; the story of the woodsman who turned his lonely farmstead into a slaughterhouse for human cattle. Real-life inspiration for films such as "Psycho" and "The Silence of the Lambs". Includes Gein biography with crime photographs, plus illustrated filmography.